MERIDIAN DAYS

Eric Brown was born in 1960 and has lived in Australia, India, and Greece. He began writing in 1975 and his first publication was a play for children, *Noel's Ark* (1982). His stories have appeared in *Interzone, Other Edens, Zenith*, and many other publications. He lives in Haworth, West Yorkshire.

Also by Eric Brown in Pan Books

The Time-Lapsed Man and Other Stories

Eric Brown

MERIDIAN DAYS

PAN BOOKS

LONDON, SYDNEY, AND AUCKLAND

First published 1992 by Pan Books Limited

This edition published 1993 by Pan Books Limited
a division of Pan Macmillan Publishers Limited
Cavaye Place London SW10 9PG
and Basingstoke

Associated companies throughout the world

ISBN 0 330 32716 X

9 8 7 6 5 4 3 2 1

A CIP catalogue record for this book is available from
the British Library

Typeset by Intype, London
Printed in England by Cox & Wyman Ltd, Reading, Berkshire

For Alex Cannon and Chris Burgess

ACKNOWLEDGEMENTS

I'd like to thank the following writers and editors for their advice and encouragement over the years: Jim Anderton, Steve Baxter, Keith Brooke, Melvin Burgess, Mike Cobley, Chris Evans, Martin Fletcher, Kathy Gale, David Garnett, Rob Holdstock, Angie Jones, Neil Jones, Bill King, Stratford Kirby, Lee Montgomery, Simon Ounsley, David Pringle, and Bob Swindells; and my agent, Antony Harwood.

MERIDIAN DAYS

1

BRIGHTSIDE

I survive.

I live from day to day – a Meridian day which humanity has created from one eternal stretch of daylight.

At night, as the floating mylar shield occludes the sun and casts its comprehensive penumbra across the archipelago, I sit on the patio and watch the pterosaurs make their way towards the beckoning aurora of Brightside. The migration of birds has always filled me with sadness and regret, a sense of being left behind. After the heat, the wind from Darkside blows, chilling me. In the early hours of darkness I often contemplate the past – even though the past is no refuge – and the series of events which brought me here.

Looking back on it, my meeting with Fire Trevellion came about quite by accident, which is how those events which change your life tend to happen. I still cannot decide whether I regret accepting Abe Cunningham's invitation to accompany him to the party thrown by the Altered artist Tamara Trevellion. The repercussions were both tragic and, for me at least, life-saving – but something visceral urged me to go, perhaps the instinct for self-preservation. I'd become something of a recluse of late, and that morning Abe must have realized that I was slipping again and in need of help. He invited me to the event to take my mind off whatever was eating me up, guilt and regret, as ever – though all Abe could see was the distance in my eyes and the leached pallor of my skin.

I'd slept badly that night, plagued by dreams of the accident. For what seemed like hours – longer, in fact, than the actual incident – I was locked in the command web of the smallship. The auxiliaries

1

were dead and I was piloting the ship through the storm on manual, with the aid of a malfunctioning computer. I relived the horror of the flight in slow-motion. As each problem arrived hard upon the last, I watched myself make the wrong decision time after time, a snowball effect of errors leading inexorably to the final catastrophe. In the nightmare I experienced again the terror I had felt at the time; not the fear of my responsibility for the hundred passengers, but the sickening dread of losing my own life. It was ironic that when I awoke screaming from the dream an instant before the impact, the terror I experienced was the remorse I carried for the dead passengers. I had emerged alive from the wreckage – if not in one piece, then with relatively minor injuries. I could be put back together, cured in body if not in mind. For the passengers, though, there was no cure.

I lay awake for a long time, staring up at the apex of the dome. I tried to get back to sleep, but images crowded in, ready to coalesce into nightmare.

I took refuge on the patio, purposefully ignoring the half-shell on the coffee table as I passed through the lounge. The warmth of the old day was tempered by a chill breeze blowing in from the tundra and ice of Darkside. In the direction of Brightside, the leading edge of the shield had slipped over the horizon, shutting out the glare of Beta Hydri. The only light came from the diamond-hard points of the stars in the void above Darkside. To east and west, the strip of sea that encircled the planet from pole to pole coruscated like a band of silver lamé. The islands of the archipelago showed as dark knobs, stretching away around the curve of the planet like the individual vertebrae of a basking leviathan. During daylight hours, the view from the dome was one of incomparable beauty, with the aurora of Brightside competing for attention with the snow-capped mountains of the sun-deprived hemisphere. At night, when the darkness was complete but for the meagre illumination of the stars, the effect was sinister. That night, the void of deep space reminded me too much of my final run.

I could not sleep, and I could not stay awake without hearing again the abbreviated screams of the passengers, so as ever there was only one thing I could do.

I returned to the lounge and emptied the contents of the half-shell into the burner. Then I carried the apparatus back to the patio and sat with it on my lap. There was a certain pre-administrative ritual to be followed, and this always had the effect of heightening the anticipation. I thought back twenty years to the summer of my sixteenth birthday, and the holiday I had taken on an island in Greece. I concentrated on the event that had made that holiday so special. Holding the image of the girl in my mind's eye, I lit the burner and inhaled the pungent fumes. What I was doing was dangerous, of course; with the visions of the accident so clear in my mind, there was always the possibility that I might pitch myself into a fugue more vivid and terrible than anything I had experienced in my nightmares. But in the event I need not have worried . . . The fumes infused my senses and reality went into a slow dissolve. Over the period of a few seconds I became oblivious of my identity, of my adult cares and worries. When I opened my eyes I was a naïve youth of sixteen again, standing on the white sands of a Mediterranean beach with all my life ahead of me. For the next eight hours I relived the bliss of that holiday; for that long I was spared the agony of guilt.

It was daylight by the time I came to my senses. The sun burned fifteen degrees above the fiery horizon of Brightside. The emptiness of the coming day was accentuated by the memories of my holiday. From time to time, as I sat on the patio and stared out across the glittering ocean to the rearing, green islands, my pulse quickened at the recollection of shared intimacies, as fresh in my mind as if I'd experienced them just yesterday; then I would realize, with a sudden sense of loss, that the love I had known was twenty years gone and as many light-years away.

I climbed unsteadily from the foam-form, staggered into the lounge and inspected the half-shell. It was empty, coated with a light dusting of powder which would have no effect at all. I checked the small wooden box I kept concealed behind the tape-case – but this, too, was empty. Part of me, the fifty per cent of Bob Benedict that knew that refuge in the drug was no salvation at all, saw this as the perfect opportunity to break my dependency. The other part, weak and irresponsible, managed to convince myself that I needed a supply of the powder on hand in case the nightmares became just *too* much; and anyway, how much stronger would be my resolve to kick the habit if I could do so while I had a supply in the dome. Happy with

3

this skewed logic, I replaced the box and decided to make the trip to Brightside in the next day or two. Then the screen chimed and my heart skipped, as if the communication were a summons from my conscience.

The lean, leonine face of my neighbour, Abe Cunningham, stared out at me. Behind him, his pterosaur hooked its scythe-like beak over his shoulder and regarded me with beady eyes.

'Bob, are you doing anything today?' The calls from a hundred exotic birds and beasts made his words indistinct.

'Actually . . . I have a couple of dozen people coming round for a party this afternoon—' I stopped myself before I began to sound too self-piteous.

Abe opened his mouth. 'Ah . . . That's a real pity. I wanted to share this twenty-five-year-old single malt I've just had Telemassed in from Earth.' He held up a chunky, old-fashioned bottle. 'You sure you can't make it?'

'Well, as a matter of fact . . . I possibly could put them off.'

Abe smiled. 'Good man. See you in an hour?'

I showered and changed, welcoming the sudden and unexpected diversion. On the way down the steps to the tiny beach and the jetty where I moored my launch, I tried to shake the lingering visions of last night's hallucination. As I cast off and steered the launch out across the open sea, the image of the girl's face receded, became indistinct, so that her features might have belonged to any one of the actresses I saw on vid-shows every day. But still, on some subconscious level, I was filled with a residual sadness, a sense of loss that even the prospect of whiling away the day at Abe's could not banish.

Reality was all very well, but it had nothing on the induced euphoria of an artificially recollected past.

I opened the throttle and accelerated across the calm flat ocean, pointing the launch in the direction of the next island in the chain. Seaspray drenched me in a cool jewelled shower. The narrow strip of sea which circumnavigated the planet was the only habitable region on the globe, and the long archipelago which straddled a quarter of the hemisphere from the north pole to the equator was where ninety-nine per cent of citizens on Meridian made their home. In the social hierarchy of the planet, Abe and myself came somewhere near the bottom; we owned small islands at the end of the chain, near the pole. The larger islands towards the equator were the exclusive province of the Altered and the Augmented, a select clique of self-styled cultural aristocrats who over the years had turned Meridian into something of a noted artists' colony.

Abe's island, despite its presumed lowly social status, was unique and, so far as I was concerned, of far more interest than the pretentiously landscaped islands owned by the wealthier citizens. Abe and his wife had arrived on Meridian ten years ago and set up a sanctuary and breeding centre for the planet's endangered species, which due to the precarious ecology of the stationary world were many. The green hump of the island was dotted with dozens of sparkling domes, like silver dewdrops in the sunlight. These were the reconstructed habitats of the planet's fauna.

Abe stood on the landing stage, hands on hips. His commanding presence was a reassuring feature of my visits to his island. He watched my approach with the pterosaur, as gaunt and beaked as Abe himself, beside him.

I tossed him the rope and he made it fast around a post, then gave me a hand from the launch. 'Bob, it's been weeks. You ought to come over more. Don't wait to be asked.'

I promised I would visit more often in future – a promise I must have made every month since my arrival on Meridian a year earlier. We strolled along the jetty and up the path towards Abe's villa on the highest point of the island. We passed domes and cages holding all manner of exotic birds and animals, the air shrill with their cries. Abe's pterosaur waddled in our wake like an obedient child.

He showed me through the dome to the verandah overlooking the stepped terracing of the island, the blue sea and the other islands stretching away into the distance. We sat in the shade on a long foam-form, and Abe made a ceremony of opening the whisky and pouring two generous measures into iced tumblers. Abe was a man of few pretensions and even fewer pleasures: Scotch – and not the drink itself so much as the occasion of its sampling – was one of his rare indulgences.

We chatted of nothing in particular for a while, the latest news from Earth, gossip from around the archipelago. Our silences were easy, periods of reflection rather than anticipation of what we might say next. Abe mentioned what he was working on now – a breeding programme involving the last surviving rabbit-analogues on the planet – and I sat back and listened, admiring the view. Flights of pterosaurs formed vortices in the distance, like computer-generated pixels illustrating thermal dynamics. On one of the larger islands, far to the south, artists competed in a smoke-sculpting contest. Towering columns, depicting mythic figures from the history of Earth, billowed in the brilliant blue sky.

I drained my first glass and Abe took great pleasure in pouring a second. Already the liquid was having an effect, making my thoughts lazy and diffuse.

In the early days of our friendship, I often wondered why Abe bothered with me. He was thirty years my senior, moderately successful at what he did, and in control of his life. As I got to know him better, I came to see that we had certain things in common. Perhaps because we were both reserved and rather introspective, we shared a suspicion of the Altereds and the Augmenteds on the higher islands. We were the only non-artists to own islands in the chain, and neither of us had capitulated to vanity and had our forms altered, either to enhance our human appearance or, as was becoming increasingly popular with a certain clique of frivolous artisans, to imitate species as varied as mythical animals and alien lifeforms. In fact, Abe wore his grey hair long and had cultivated a paunch over the past few months, as if in defiance of prevailing somatic aesthetics. Nor were we Augmented – the small occipital computer I had at the base of my skull, which I had used to interface with the controls of my smallship, was sealed now and redundant. We had only our own intellect to fall back on, unlike the Augmenteds who wore computers like yokes and spent much of their time wired into some abstract metaphysical realm at many removes from everyday reality.

Perhaps another reason for his friendliness was the fact that just over a year ago he had lost his wife in an accident on Brightside. It had happened a month before my arrival; Abe, understandably, had never mentioned the incident. All I knew was what I heard secondhand from acquaintances in common, and all *they* knew was that, in the aftermath of the accident, Abe had rushed his wife to a hospital on Main Island, but by the time he arrived she was beyond help.

There were a number of pictures of Patricia Cunningham in the villa: a smiling, fair-haired woman in her early fifties. Other showed Abe and Patricia together: they had seemed a happy couple, and I'd often caught myself wondering if having someone and losing them was more terrible than never having had anyone at all.

Occasionally, while wasting time in the isolation of my own dome, I thought of the widower in his hilltop eyrie. He was just as isolated as I was, with his Scotch and his memories, and I frequently felt bad about not taking up his offer of open house. But the guilt never lasted all that long: I had my own memories, and my own means of dealing with them.

'You really should stop me going on like this,' Abe said, at the end of a rambling monologue on the subject of his latest project. 'No wonder you don't come up here so often. I'm sorry – I'm a fauna bore.'

Beside him, the pterosaur stropped its bill on an extended wing. I gestured and said something to the effect that I enjoyed hearing about his work; which was true. Listening to the details of other people's lives, I temporarily forget those of my own.

'What have you been doing with yourself recently?' Abe asked. 'How's work?'

I shrugged, suddenly defensive. When asked to account for my own activities, I found myself for once viewing my life with some degree of objectivity, and I was never enamoured with what I saw.

'Nothing much. Business is bad – I haven't had any work in months.'

Before becoming a pilot in my early twenties, I had overhauled fliers and shuttles for the Javelin Line. When I arrived on Meridian, I fell back on this skill and set myself up in business as a mechanic. For a few months I'd been patronized by rich artists and their friends – the one-time smallship pilot, down on his luck – but the sympathy had soon dried up and with it the supply of fliers in need of repair.

Abe listened, hands clasped behind his head. 'If there's anything I can do, Bob . . .' He trailed off, then peered at me. 'If you don't mind me saying so, you look terrible. You sure you're OK?'

I laughed, but it rang hollow in my ears. 'I'm OK, Abe. I'm just run down, that's all. I haven't been sleeping.'

Abe knew about the accident. Months ago I'd given him the story – the sanitized, emotion-free version, that is. As far as he was aware,

I was just a blameless pawn in a smallship blow-out. He knew nothing about my guilt and the need to suppress it, and what I did to do so. He knew nothing about my dependency.

There were times when I wanted to tell him everything, as if to absolve myself from blame, but I feared his censure and valued his occasional company too much to risk losing it.

The pterosaur regarded me accusingly. The staple diet of these birds was the flower of the thorned cacti which grew on Brightside and which they consumed without any side-effects.

'Bob, how would you like to go to a party tonight?'

'Well, to be honest . . .'

'I've been invited to an "event" down in the archipelago. I wasn't going to go, but it might be interesting . . . You do need to get out, you know.'

I tried to think of an excuse, but came up with nothing. I temporized. 'What is this "event", exactly?' I disliked the way every novice artisan and ambitious technician graced their shows and exhibitions with the soubriquet of *event*.

Abe tried not to smile. 'It's a combined poetry recital and film show. It might be good. And anyway, even if it isn't, the fact remains that you need a change of scenery. The guests won't all be Altereds and Augmenteds. There'll be a whole crowd of techs from the Telemass station, along for the free drinks.'

I was still casting about for an excuse not to attend.

'Who's the artist?' I asked.

'Have you heard of the sculptress and poet Tamara Trevellion?'

'Wasn't she . . . ?'

Abe nodded. 'You probably saw her on the news last year, when she lost her husband. She's an Altered fish-woman.'

I watched little news – most of it was from Earth, and that planet held bad memories for me – but I had caught the news flash reporting the Telemass accident. Three citizens had been mistranslated and lost somewhere along the Earth–Meridian vector, with little hope of recovery.

The tragedy became even more sensational when it was announced that Maximilian Trevellion, the famous crystal artist, was one of the missing persons. Tamara Trevellion was interviewed, and she turned the performance into an 'event' worthy of her finest creative endeavour. Few who watched her could fail to be moved by the poise and valour of the mer-woman as she told the world that now, after three days, she acknowledged that her husband was lost but that his spirit and his work would live on both in her heart and in the minds of those who appreciated true art.

Later, the tragedy was compounded when it was disclosed that the trip to Earth taken by her husband, to represent Tamara Trevellion at a reading of one of her prose-poems, was to have been made by her daughter, Fire. At the last moment, Fire Trevellion had fallen ill, and Maximilian had taken the fateful trip instead.

'Well?' Abe asked now. 'I was told to bring someone. You're more than welcome to come along.'

'Do you know Tamara Trevellion?' I tried to conceal my surprise that the artist should wish to socialize with a lowly conservationist.

'I've supplied her with a number of exotic pets over the years,' Abe said. 'Well?'

I recalled again the tragic mask of beauty and her brave soliloquy at the loss of a loved one, and I wondered how the passage of time had treated Tamara Trevellion. This, and the fact that I knew Abe was right when he said that I needed to get out more, overcame my resistance.

I nodded. 'Why not?'

Abe smiled, poured more whisky and began a speech to the effect that the best Scotch was still made on Earth. We chatted about our home planet for a time. 'By the way,' Abe said, 'the last time we met you were talking of going back.'

I shrugged. 'The thought does cross my mind from time to time, I must admit. I like it here, but—'

'But Earth is home, right? So what's stopping you? The fact that Earth still has smallships?'

I looked up. Abe was casually stroking the bill of his pterosaur. He knew he'd scored a hit.

'OK, maybe that does have something to do with it.'

Earth still used smallships on all the in-system runs, and I knew that the sight of one would release a whole slew of unwelcome memories and associations. At the same time, the reason I told people that I intended to return to Earth one day was so that I might build a psychological momentum and eventually match my words with the deed, escape from what was keeping me on Meridian.

Still regarding the bird, Abe said, 'Bob, you remind me a lot of Terror, here. I saw him being driven from his flock one day and found him down on the beach, injured and forlorn. I've no idea what he did to get himself ostracized like that. He's fit now and perfectly able to leave here – but, as you see, he won't . . . Perhaps he's too scared to return and face his past.'

'So you think my talk of going back is no more than just that – talk?'

Abe shrugged. 'I think you'd be a damned sight better off if you returned to where you really belonged.'

I was saved from having to reply – if I could have found a suitable response – by the sound of Abe's vid-screen chiming in the lounge. He excused himself, entered the dome and activated the wall-screen. The picture showed an expanse of sand, clearly Brightside, shimmering in a vaporous heat haze. I made out a cage in the foreground, containing an animal.

I turned my attention to the view of the island chain and contemplated Abe's words. I had assumed until now that I had kept my feelings concerning the accident pretty well concealed – but Abe was more astute a judge of human nature than I had given him credit for. Perhaps I should have felt gladdened at his concern, but instead I felt almost threatened.

Abe returned a minute later. 'That was a remote sensor I have monitoring a cage. I've just trapped the female of a species I hope to breed in captivity.' He glanced at his watch. 'I really must go and collect it. There'll be time to get there and back before the party starts.'

'Is the cage on Brightside?'

'A hundred kilometres in. It'll be a hot trip.'

I tried to sound casual. 'Any chance of a ride?'

He looked surprised, then pleased. I was not known to exhibit such camaraderie. 'I don't see why not. I could use a hand with the cage. Ever been Brightside before?'

'No,' I lied. 'I'd like the experience.'

He nodded. 'I've a spare silversuit somewhere.'

*

As we kitted-up in the solar-reflective silversuits, water-cooled but light and flexible, I felt a twinge of guilt at deceiving him like this. I salved my conscience with the resolve that this would be the start of a closer friendship with Abe Cunningham.

Abe's flier was a sleek silver tear-drop, at rest on the harbour wall but pointing as if in readiness towards Brightside. He opened the wing hatches and we dropped inside. The padded, insulated interior, darkened by the tinted viewscreen and fitted out with hi-tech instruments, brought to mind the pilot's nacelle of a smallship.

Abe gunned the engine; the jets caught and we streaked away from the island, a metre above the calm surface of the sea.

A computer screen embedded in the dashboard showed a circular view of the Brightside hemisphere. It was divided into three zones, like a target. Abe explained. 'The outer margin is zone blue, the coolest area, suitable for human habitation. The second ring, extending for a couple of hundred kilometres, is zone orange, where you go only if you have good reason. The inner core, zone red, is strictly a no-go area. We're here—' He indicated a small flashing light moving towards the outer circle. 'And the cage is here—' A second point of light well within zone orange.

We would be venturing further into the zone of fire than ever I had before.

Ahead, on the horizon, Brightside appeared as a low line just above sea level, shimmering in the convection currents. The sky above the distant landmass was white hot, leached of colour by the incessant and merciless radiation of the sun. Few people, other than the occasional research team, ventured far into this sunward-facing hemisphere; no one had yet made a Brightside crossing. On the equator, the mantle of rock over an area of a thousand square kilometres had formed a hellish lagoon of molten lava. Even the most hardy of the planet's fauna dwelled within the safety margin of zone blue, beside the meridional ocean.

One hour later we were still kilometres from the ochreous foreshore of the Brightside, and the thermometer on the dash indicated that the temperature outside was 110°F. Every breath of air, seemingly devoid of oxygen, parched my throat. I took frequent drinks from Abe's canteen.

He leaned forward and peered through the viewscreen, then pointed. 'Look . . .'

I followed his gesture. To our left, high in the blue sky above the ocean, a falling bolt of white light appeared suddenly as if by magic. The first bolt, to which Abe had alerted me, had already found its target, the great arched column reducing in length as it hit the Telemass reception pad. The second bolt followed instantly, then a third, all landing on the largest island of the chain some two hundred kilometres south of our present position. Each pulse, from its first appearance in the stratosphere to the time it hit destination, lasted for barely a second, and as ever I found it hard to believe that I had witnessed the medium which transported the constituent molecules of human beings and supplies more than twenty light-years through space from Earth to Meridian. I found it even more difficult to accept that I too had undergone the same process of reduction, transmission, and reconstitution.

'The sight always gives me one hell of a thrill.'

Abe smiled. 'You're not alone. I think everyone feels the same. I know I do. And it's not just our intellect trying to come to terms with the technological wonder of it.'

I was staring to my left, imagining the sensation of dislocation and relief that the travellers would be experiencing as they were re-formed on the deck of the station.

'We always feel awe at that which we don't understand,' Abe was saying. 'But it's more than that. When we see the bolts, we're reminded of the connection to Earth. It's the lifeline to the one place we all have in common. The sight of the bolts reassures us that mother Earth still cares, that we're still connected by the techno-umbilical that gave us our new life here.'

'Hence the massive news coverage when something goes wrong, like the mistranslation last year?'

He nodded. A thousand droplets of sweat stood out on his face. 'And hence the concern over recent rumours concerning the station.'

There were times when my isolation and indifference to what was happening outside the confines of my head put me at a serious disadvantage. 'What rumours?'

'You haven't heard?' Abe glanced quickly from the viewscreen to me. 'There's been a reduction of staffing levels at the station over the past couple of months. The Director's leaving soon for a more prestigious posting. Rumour is that both incoming and outgoing shots will be cut to one a month.'

'But it's just that, I take it? A rumour?' At present, there were three shots to and from Earth every month.

'It's a rumour Director Steiner hasn't bothered to deny, Bob. On a broadcast last week he was non-committal. If it is true, it'll probably mean a waiting list and one hell of a price increase. I'm glad I don't send that much to Earth, but some of the artists will not be pleased.' I thought I detected a slight note of irony in his tone.

'Meridian isn't that popular any more,' I commented.

'Tourism's down fifty per cent since last year, after the quake scare. A dozen big hotels on Main have shut up shop over the past six months. Also, Consolidated Mining has got what it can from the margins of Brightside and Darkside – they reckon increased investment to go further in wouldn't be a sound proposition. Earth is looking to other, bigger colonies for investment, hence the rumours of scale-down.' Abe laughed. 'We'll soon be a backwater, Bob. Here we go.'

We had reached the parched plains of Brightside. Abe accelerated and we rocketed at great speed across the wastes of the comparatively safe zone blue. In three directions, for as far as the eye could see, the land ran flat and featureless, but for the occasional rock the size of a fist and even smaller ground-hugging plants. The seared air above the distant horizon wavered like a film projected on to a corrugated screen.

We followed a rough track inland, a slight linear depression made by the vehicles which had passed this way before us. I was thankful for the flier's sun-roof and our silversuits. On my previous trips to Brightside, quick sorties to get what I wanted with not a second wasted, my launch had been uncovered and I had forgone the luxury of a cooled suit – and I had returned every time exhausted and dehydrated.

As we advanced across zone blue, an area about as hospitable as the Sahara in mid-summer, the temperature hit 130°. Even in the shade of the cab the heat parched my skin, and each breath seared my throat.

We raced over extensive rafts of cacti-like flora; I recognized the bright pink blooms, and wished we could stop so I could gather the flowers and return. Then we travelled for kilometres without seeing any sign of vegetation, and I began to despair that we had passed the last of the growth, that the trip would be wasted. We bore remorselessly on, speeding towards the great incandescent orb of the sun burning relentlessly fifteen degrees above the horizon, as if intent on immolating ourselves.

A while later, I thought I detected something in the distance. It was a slight irregularity, growing line by line from the shimmering horizon like the build-up of lateral graphics on a computer screen. As we approached, the image resolved itself: a building, a white-panelled, monolithic ziggurat out of place here in the middle of nowhere.

Abe slowed the flier and we idled alongside. Behind a high wire-mesh fence, the giant lettering on the façade of the building proclaimed: SOLAR RE ... while the remainder of the sign, SEARCH STATION, hung at an angle across the entrance. Radio dishes and antennas on the building's roof were pointing at the sun like so many heliotropic blooms. The station had about it an air of terminal desolation; the very fact that the roof-top instruments were still directed at the subject of the research made the abandonment all the more forlorn.

'Shut down three months ago,' Abe said, 'when Earth turned off the funding.'

We accelerated and the dead station receded in our wake, the flashing point on the screen before us indicating that we were leaving zone blue behind us.

Brightside, zone orange ...

Abe cut the engine. The flier settled. For a second, the sand displaced by our landing masked the merciless glare of Beta Hydri. Then the cloud settled, and the white hot disc of the sun reappeared. A wall of fire reared on the horizon, a dancing curtain of golden light which erupted frequently in great incandescent gouts of flame. As we stared through the viewscreen, the silver paint on the hood of the flier began to flake. The thermometer read 180°.

We had come to rest on a baked plain of sand beside an outcropping of rocks and boulders – the habitat of the rabbit-analogue that

Abe had ensnared. Ten metres in front of the flier was the cage, a small, furless shape within it.

Then, beyond it, I saw the cacti.

They spread for as far as the eye could see, a dense matt of green, spatulate vegetation dotted here and there with pink flowers. The sight filled me with joy.

All I had to do now was snatch them without Abe noticing . . .

I had no doubt that he knew the blooms were the source of the powerful mnemonic-hallucinogenic drug so popular with the colonists in the early days, before the expensive designer-pharmaceuticals hit the market. Abe had been too long on Meridian to be in ignorance of the fact. But there was no way he might know of my dependency, and I had no intention of letting him find out. He was solicitous enough about my welfare as it was, without attempting to save me from the one thing that made my life bearable.

'Gloves and hood,' he was saying. 'Don't forget the face mask, and don't look directly at the sun. We're going to spend as little time out there as possible. We'll stow the cage away, then it's back in here, OK?'

'Fine by me,' I lied, my heart sinking. I pulled on the gloves, arranged the hood and the face mask.

'OK,' Abe said. 'Let's go . . .'

He opened the hatches and we climbed out.

The heat of the sun hit me with the force of a physical blow. I felt myself bowing beneath it. The miniature refrigeration unit on my back began a laboured whirring as it fought to keep the circulating water cool.

We walked towards the cage, two silversuited figures in an alien, hostile land. To all sides, the ground only as far as the mid-distance was visible; further afield was the shimmering optical illusion of convection currents, giving the paradoxical impression that we were surrounded by large areas of water. My mind switched to thoughts of swimming pools and long, iced drinks.

The nearest cacti plant was some metres beyond the cage, and I was wondering how I might reach it unseen when Abe stopped me with an arm across my chest. 'Bob! Back in the cab – there's a laser. Quick!'

I ran, ignorance of Abe's alarm lending panic to my flight. I reached the cab, exhausted, unclipped the laser from the door-rack.

Abe was running back to meet me.

'What the hell—?' I began.

He grabbed the rifle. 'Look . . .'

Perhaps a hundred metres beyond the cage was the hulking, armoured shape of a sand lion, the size and weight of a dump truck. I had only ever seen them on vid-documentaries, great quadrupeds resembling a cross between a prehistoric triceratops and a rhino. Even at this distance the clashing of its mandibles rang loud in my ears.

'Christ, Bob . . .'

He passed a pair of binoculars to me, and only when I raised them and sighted the lion did I understand the reason for his distress.

The animal was devouring what once might have been a human being. Now the figure was stiff and lifeless, an oversized rag-doll in the fanged jaws of the lion. The carcass was parcelled in the remains of a familiar light-blue uniform . . .

I lowered the binoculars, and the intervening distance made the sight of the carnage almost bearable. The sound remained though, the clash of fangs and the eager, liquid sucking as it feasted. Within seconds, there was very little left of the corpse.

Abe and I were still staring like prize fools when the lion looked up and saw us. There was a second's hesitation before the animal decided that it was not yet sated. Then it charged.

Sand lions, I recalled from the vid-programme, were notoriously difficult to kill. High velocity bullets could penetrate the inch-thick armour, but bullets were an antique ammunition no longer available on Meridian. Laser bolts could at best only stun the beasts. I recalled the deaths of three scientists on Brightside just six months ago, attacked and devoured by a pair of the man-eaters. I had thought, then, that it was a particularly horrible way to go . . .

The lion trundled towards us, gaining momentum as it came. It had lowered its great hanging head, presenting a crest of horns and spikes. Its stench reached us in advance, the heady stink of putrescent carrion and an acid odour peculiar to the beast. I yelled out in fear.

Deliberately, Abe raised his rifle and fired. The electric-blue bolt sizzled across the gap, actually connecting the hunter to the hunted for a fraction of a second. The bolt slammed into the ridge of osseous armour-plating above the animal's brow. It dropped a matter of metres from us with a great grunt of expelled air.

'Bob!' Abe cried.

But I had seen my opportunity and was taking it.

I ran past the felled beast; a swarm of flies rose from it, and minute parasites swam in the film of oil that covered its chitinous exoskeleton. I had no idea how long the lion might remain unconscious, and in retrospect I realized what a fool I was. But at the time I had thoughts for only one thing. When I reached the remains, a scattered collection of rags and bones, I knelt and snatched a fragment of blue uniform, along with as many small pink flower-heads as I could manage without Abe's getting wise.

Then I sprinted back past the lion; it was still unconscious, but twitching spasmodically and growling as if gradually coming to its senses.

'Bob – that was a bloody fool trick!'

I thrust the scraps of blue uniform at him. He took it, looked up at me. 'A Telemass tech . . .' Then he remembered himself. 'Quick, let's get the cage aboard.'

Between us, keeping one eye on the concussed lion, we lifted the cage and carried it back to the flier. The darkened, cooled interior of the cab was like an ice-box in comparison to the hell we had just escaped. Abe dogged the hatches and sat back in relief. I peeled off my gloves and removed my mask.

'That was a foolish thing to do, Bob.'

'I had to get it . . .'

Abe unfolded the blood-stained material on his lap, revealing the Telemass logo – three scimitars, points touching.

'But what the hell was he doing out this far, Bob? He didn't stand a chance . . .'

He looked up, through the viewscreen, out to the scatter of bones in the desert. 'If he came out here alone,' he went on, 'then where's his vehicle? And if he didn't, then someone knows something about this.'

He drew a deep breath, folded the rag with reverence and tucked it into his pouch.

The sand lion was stirring, attempting to gain its feet. Abe fired the jets, swung the flier around on its axis and headed towards home.

We made the return trip without a word, our long shadow streaking ahead of us. Beside me, Abe seemed lost in thought; it came to me that what we had witnessed today served only to remind Abe of another death, this one much closer to him, that had occurred on Brightside over a year ago. I could think of nothing to say, so I kept quiet. It was a relief to come upon the cool blue ocean of the meridian again, and leave the nightmare of Brightside behind us.

Only when we reached Abe's island did he speak. 'I'll get on to Steiner, tell him about it.' He smiled wearily. 'See you tonight, Bob.'

I collected my launch and steered it back to my island. I climbed the path to the dome, entered the lounge and stood in silence for a long time, contemplating the empty half-shell. Normally, I would have set to work immediately and prepared the drug, but the thought of doing that now, while Abe remained alone with his memories, deterred me. I threw the desiccated flower-heads into a corner, showered and changed for the party.

2

FIRE AND FROST

The archipelago – the collection of two hundred islands inhabited by perhaps a hundred thousand citizens – straddled one of the many fault lines which circumnavigated the planet. Situated between the infernal pressures of Brightside and the contracting frigidity of Darkside, the islands suffered regular earthquakes. On an average of once a year, the quake-warning siren wailed its ugly double note and we prepared ourselves for the imminent upheaval. In the course of the colony's twenty-five years, no fewer than five new islands had emerged from the depths, and three had tumbled back into the ocean. Meridian was not the safest planet in the Expansion, but perhaps this was what attracted the community of artists to the archipelago, the desire to live a precarious existence balanced between sublime beauty and the constant threat of annihilation.

Tamara and Maximilian Trevellion had been even more daring than most: they had purchased one of the more recent additions to the island chain. According to Abe, the island had been nothing more than a lifeless nub of rock twenty years ago when Trevellion and her husband arrived on Meridian and saw, with the imagination and foresight of the artists they were, the potential of the barren rock. They had landscaped the island with a riot of local vegetation and supervised the construction of a luxurious living-dome on its highest point.

It was nine when we arrived. Abe steered his flier into a marina packed with the expensive yachts and power-boats of the rich and famous. I began to feel uneasy at the thought of socializing with the Altered and Augmented artists. They were renowned for their snobbery, their élitist disdain of those who were neither Altered nor

Augmented. I wished that I had made some excuse after all and remained at home.

One of a dozen uniformed attendants supervising the mooring of the vessels made the flier fast and we stepped on to the quayside.

The day was still light. The sun burned just above the horizon with the same unremitting ferocity as it had at midday. Trevellion's dome, high on the hilltop, was illuminated with interior neons in preparation for the swift fall of night, due in one hour with the arrival of the orbital shield. It could be seen on the horizon to the north, a dark, edge-on meniscus moving slowly towards the archipelago.

Other guests alighted from their boats and strolled along the marble quayside, men and women from all three social castes, dressed as if for some prestigious award ceremony. I noticed the number of guards stationed around the marina and standing sentry along the zig-zag path which led up to the dome. They wore black uniforms and carried laser rifles, and their presence at what was supposed to be an artistic event struck me as bizarre. I recalled the story that soon after her husband's death, a year ago, Tamara Trevellion had hired her own private army to police the island and protect the many works of art on open show.

A tall *maître d'* in a scarlet uniform with chunky epaulettes took Abe's invitation card, scanned us and indicated the escalator.

As we took our place on the moving stairway, Abe glanced across at me. He must have sensed my apprehension. 'Hey, Bob. Don't worry. We have business here, after all. I couldn't get through to Steiner this afternoon, so I left a message. I did get through to Inspector Foulds, though. He said he'd talk to us tonight.'

We arrived at the entrance to the dome. A doorman ushered us through the foyer and across a luxuriously furnished lounge, to a cupola'd exit which gave on to a vast landscaped lawn thronged with guests. As we stepped outside, our names and professions – I was introduced as an ex-starship pilot – issued from a concealed speaker. Heads turned briefly, but the hubbub of conversation continued without pause.

The lawn was furnished with numerous works of arts, striking laser sculptures and statues in bronze and platinum – the work of the late Maximilian Trevellion. Behind us, others guests were announced and made their entries – some evidently big names, if

the lull in conversation was any indication. At one point a polite
patter of applause greeted the arrival of an Augmented artist, who
took a bow in acknowledgement. The guests were deployed across
the lawn in groups according to their castes – at this early stage the
consumption of alcohol or drugs had yet to dismantle the social
barriers. Many cliques were gathered around burners on pedestals,
inhaling the euphor-fumes. A live band pulsed out a selection of
electro-classics from across the Expansion. In the saddle-shaped
greensward adjacent to the lawn, I made out two large oval screens
floating in the air; technicians on grav-sleds hovered beside them,
hurriedly applying the finishing touches. I assumed that the illuminated meadow was the venue for tonight's event.

We stood at the edge of the lawn, and I stared with wonder at the
gathering. This was the first time I had been among so many Altered
and Augmenteds, and I felt an extreme reluctance to mix. On Main
Island, the only sizeable town on the archipelago, the majority of
citizens on the streets were normals – or primitives, as we were
known. The A's were too busy creating their masterpieces to be seen
during the day, and anyway they had servants to do their errands.
They came out at night, to be seen at the most expensive restaurants
and exclusive parties.

The Augmenteds were relatively unspectacular. They were essen-
tially primitives, wired with the latest cerebro-assist mechanisms,
occipital auxiliaries and forearm key-pads. The technology had
reached such a level of sophistication that many assists could have
been miniaturized and worn unobtrusively – but that would have
defeated the purpose of being seen as Augmented. The art these
people produced had more in common with quantum physics and
higher mathematics than any recognizable form of art a mere normal
like myself might appreciate.

The Altereds, on the other hand, were *radically* different. Many
had had themselves transformed totally, with only tell-tale, vestigial
characteristics to indicate their original humanity – altered so that
they exhibited the outward appearance of beasts both extinct and
extant, Terran and alien. One woman had gone the whole hog, so
to speak, and taken on the soma-form of an overweight sow, with
only her beautiful face remaining, incongruously pert on so solid a
neck. I heard her discussing three-dimensional cubism with an

21

orang-utang-man. I saw many other guests so changed and, to my eyes, ugly, that I could only assume they had adopted extra-terrestrial forms.

There were a few normals to be seen here and there: one group stood around a euphor-burner, laughing among themselves. I saw a few Telemass techs, in the light-blue uniforms of the Organization, and a number of business people from Main Island.

As Abe and I moved to the edge of the lawn and admired the view of a beach far below, with the ocean and the other islands beyond, one normal from a nearby group disengaged himself and walked over to us. He was laughing off the effects of the fumes.

'Abraham, Bob – good to see you both.'

Douglas Foulds was a square, powerful man in his early fifties. He was from the colony planet of Baxter's Landfall, a world with a greater gravity than either Earth or Meridian, and in comparison to the other guests he seemed ridiculously squat and compacted. Doug was Meridian's Chief Inspector of police: with a couple of dozen men under him to do the leg-work, he was largely desk-bound. Not that this ever prevented him from attending all the big parties and social functions on the archipelago.

'Hell, Abe – why don't you two mix a little? Here, I'll introduce you to a few friends of mine.'

Doug had called in on me soon after my arrival on Meridian, and during the course of the next few months we had become friends. We found we had the sport of power-gliding in common, and we had spent many a weekend exploring the meridian. A combination of his work, and my increased drug dependency, had meant that over the past six months I had hardly seen him. On the odd occasion that he had called me, suggesting that we hit the skies sometime, I had put him off with lame excuses.

Now he stood between us, hardly reaching our shoulders. He gripped our elbows and escorted us across the lawn like a jailer.

A horde of Altereds stood around a euphor-pedestal by the entrance of the dome, high on a combination of the fumes and champagne. The air was thick with good-natured banter and the frequent explosion of laughter.

'Dougy!' someone – or rather *something* – roared, as we invaded the territory of the herd. '*Do* introduce us to your friends!' This sounded all the more threatening because the speaker had the magnificent head of a lion.

'Abe, Bob,' Doug said, 'meet the Tamara Trevellion fan-club. Boys and girls, Abe and Bob.' He indicated the lion-man. 'Leo Realisto. Leo's perhaps the finest performance artist on the planet.'

The Altered demurred, fingers to his pink cravat. I counted a dozen animal types in the group, but these differed from the other Altereds I had seen tonight in that they had retained their upright postures – only their heads, and in some cases torsos, having undergone the transformation. Leo Realisto wore a white three-piece suit, and this sophistication of attire served to make incongruous and even startling his majestic leonine head and golden mane.

We circulated. Doug introduced us to all types of Altered; from the domestic and mundane dog and cat, to the more exotic armadillo, mandrill, and zebra. From the neck down, all were immaculately outfitted in the latest designer fashions, and I could almost convince myself that they were sporting ingenious headpieces, but for the verisimilitude of their slavering chops and facial mucous membranes.

'These people are admirers of Tamara Trevellion,' Doug told us. 'She was the first person to go in for full body transformation, and their partial alterations are in homage. After all, it would be *passé* to go all the way . . . Ah, Trixi!'

He stood on tip-toe and waved to a petite girl almost as short as himself. She waved frantically in return, rushed over and hugged him. She had the head of what I assumed was a bush-baby – large, dark eyes, a small pink snout and facial fur marked with chevrons of white. The rest of her body was that of an athletic eighteen-year-old, and the total effect of the combination was, I thought, rather grotesque.

'A pilot!' she shrilled, when Doug introduced us. She clapped a hand over her huge eyes. 'But, oh! Too *technical*!' She gave a shiver of delicious terror. 'May I?'

Before I could stop her, she reached out and ran her fingers through the hair at the back of my head, her wet nose a matter of centimetres from my face. She located my occipital console. 'Too much!' she squealed. 'But, oh, how *can* you? All those little machiney bits in your head!'

'It's sealed,' I said, and chastised myself for sounding so defensive.

'But *still*!' the bush-baby cried.

I think Doug sensed my unease. He grabbed a floating tray of drinks and offered them around. 'Anyway, what brings you here tonight, Bob? Heard about Trevellion's event?'

'I was doing nothing better.' I shrugged. 'What is the event?'

'You don't know? Think about it. What's today?' Doug and Trixi stood with their arms about each other, smiling up at us.

I exchanged a mystified glance with Abe.

Doug laughed. 'Tell them, Trixi.'

The bush-baby, rocking her head from side to side with each word like a metronome, carolled, 'It's exactly a year to the day since Tamara Trevellion lost her husband in the Telemass accident!'

'Those in the know are expecting something big to commemorate the tragedy,' Doug said. 'It should be quite a show.'

Abe looked around. 'Has Trevellion shown herself yet?'

Doug chuckled, his startlingly blue eyes wide under a full head of grey curls. He was high from the euphor-fumes which swirled around our heads. I was beginning to feel a little woozy myself – or perhaps it was the company. 'She's probably rehearsing her triumphal entry. I presume you've heard the latest?'

'Some of us do have full-time occupations,' Abe chided.

'Grossly unfair!' Doug said. 'The gathering of intelligence is all in the line of duty, after all.'

'So what's the latest?' Abe prompted.

Doug winked. 'I've heard that Trevellion's taken Wolfe Steiner as her lover.'

Trixi covered her mouth. 'Coo, weird!' she giggled.

'Well, it is a year since she lost her husband,' I began in Trevellion's defence.

'Oh, don't get me wrong – I have nothing against her seeing anyone,' Doug said. 'But Wolfe Steiner?'

Trixi wrinkled her nose. 'Wolfe!' she cried. 'Yech, the Ice-man!'

Abe frowned. 'I don't understand your objection. I know he's Augmented, but . . .' It was a rare event for Altereds to consort with Augmenteds, and vice versa, but not unknown.

Doug was shaking his head. 'Hear me out, Abe. Don't you think it a little odd, Trevellion's having an affair with the Director of the Telemass station, just a year after the accident?'

Abe shrugged. 'I don't really see . . .'

'You don't know Trevellion,' Doug said. 'She's a cold fish – pun intentional. She was distraught last year, grief-stricken. She swore she'd never get over the loss of Max. If you recall, she even threatened to sue Steiner for negligence.'

'But the inquiry cleared him,' I began.

'That's beside the point. Whatever his involvement, Trevellion held him responsible. That makes their liaison now all the more suspicious.'

I considered telling Doug that the lack of opportunity to play the real detective on Meridian was forcing him to imagine intrigue where none existed.

'Perhaps,' Abe suggested, 'Trevellion has seen the error of her ways, found Steiner to be a thoroughly decent guy, and fallen in love with him.'

'Don't give me any of that romantic bullshit, Abe! I've been around long enough to know when something smells . . . *fishy*,' and he chuckled again at his pun. Trixi joined in.

Abe took the opportunity to change the subject. 'Talking about Steiner,' he said, 'I couldn't contact him today about what happened on Brightside. Is he likely to be here tonight?'

'He'll no doubt be dancing attendance to Trevellion,' Doug said. He kissed Trixi on her pink snout and patted her bottom. 'Run along, now. There's a good girl.' He turned to us. 'About those remains . . .' he said when Trixi had scampered away. He seemed reluctant to discuss work when there was a party to enjoy.

In the event he was saved the effort.

We were interrupted by the arrival of the night-time phase. The leading edge of the oval shield swooped over the island, bringing with it the brief twilight which presaged eight hours of total darkness. Towards the sunward horizon, the shield was drawing slowly across the burning orb like a great shutter. With the advent of the penumbra, the Brightside aurora burned all the more magnificently, creating spectacular reflections on the surface of the sea. There was a spontaneous burst of applause from the guests on the lawn. Trevellion's dome glowed in the gathering darkness, and from nowhere a spotlight flashed on, picking out the arched exit and the steps leading down to the garden.

'What did I tell you?' Doug murmured in satisfaction.

The music grew muted. A hush descended over the gathering, and the Altereds beside us gazed up in adoration. Tamara Trevellion made her entry.

I stared, too, but the emotion I experienced was more revulsion than reverence. I thought at first that she was wearing a sheer black evening gown. But then I saw, as she paused in the spotlight at the top of the stairs a matter of metres from us, that I was mistaken. Tamara Trevellion was entirely naked. The gown was in fact a membranous series of frills and fins which flowed and eddied around her body like the finest filigree. Her breasts had been removed, her vagina concealed behind a flap of scales. But it was her face that I found more shocking. Thin lips hyphenated mailed cheeks, and her eyes were huge, grey and depthless. A high, spined crest began at her brow and carried on over her narrow skull to the nape of her neck. Gills, sealed now, were angry red incisions at her throat. The entire effect – far from being aesthetically pleasing, as I guessed had been her intention – was monstrous. I recalled the beautiful mer-woman I had seen on my vid-screen a year ago, and could not decide if my senses had been at fault, or if Trevellion had had herself further Altered.

'The Black Widow fish of the Darkside deeps,' Abe whispered to me, staring at her. 'Its pigment blackens for camouflage when the male of the species has fertilized it and died.'

I stared up at the tall, regal figure. I had to admit that I found her imposing, perhaps because of the way she stood, immobile and silent, regarding her guests as if we were her subjects.

Only then did I notice the two people standing in her wake. One was a small, thin girl, who I took to be her maid or companion. I was immediately taken by her: she was dressed rather plainly, as if she had had the yellow smock selected for her, rather than having chosen it herself – but this served only to highlight her natural prettiness. She was the first woman I had seen that evening who seemed wholly natural and *human*. I wondered if Trevellion had had a say in the girl's attire, so as not to be upstaged by her maid.

The second figure was a fat, bald-headed man who I recognized from news broadcasts as Trevellion's surgeon, responsible for her alteration. He hovered close behind the fish-woman like some kind of piscean parasite, as if expecting his skills to be called upon at any second.

'Ladies and gentlemen,' Trevellion began in a clear, cold soprano, lights flashing off her iridescent scales. 'I am, of course, honoured by your presence. Today is somewhat special for me, as you well know. It came to me that the occasion could not go without some form of event to mark it, a creation of surpassing merit. To this end, for the past month, I have endeavoured to create a montage with commentary for your appreciation. The piece is entitled "Memoriam" and will be screened, as ever, above the greensward in a little over thirty minutes. I sincerely hope you enjoy.' A round of applause greeted the words, and I found myself joining in. Trevellion raised her hands in an imperious gesture, demanding silence. 'Perhaps at this point, I might take the opportunity to mention that I have arranged a special live event to be performed next week . . .' At this, a murmur of appreciation spread through the audience. 'I have been planning this event for some months now, and modestly believe it to be my finest creation. As yet untitled, it will symbolize Earth's relationship with Meridian. You are all invited.' Trevellion inclined her head. 'Thank you.' More applause, and accepting it like royalty she stepped from the spotlight and circulated, the girl and the surgeon in close attendance.

'Well,' Doug commented, 'that should be worth the wait. Trevellion's live events are quite something.' He broke off and gestured to someone among a group of Augmenteds.

Across the lawn Wolfe Steiner was engaged in conversation with a short, bearded man. When he saw Doug he excused himself with a civil bow and joined us. He towered over Doug, the effect of the two men side by side almost comical. The Director of the Telemass Organization was attired in a severe black uniform; his silver hair, cropped short. emphasized his military bearing.

'Inspector Foulds.' He inclined his Augmented head towards the officer, then to Abe and myself.

'Wolfe,' Doug said jovially, and the use of his first name was like a challenge, 'enjoying the party?' I was suddenly aware of a charge of ill-feeling between the Director and the Inspector.

Unsmiling, the Director tipped his head to one side in a noncommittal gesture. 'As parties go, it is above the average.'

'We don't usually see you at these events,' Doug went on.

'I have been especially busy of late.'

I wondered if Director Steiner's air of detachment – although bodily present, he seemed absent, as if he had left his personality elsewhere – was the result of some belligerence between Doug and himself, or an effect of his Augmentation. Many Augmenteds I had met seemed to exist in a realm at one remove from reality, lost like autistics in some private inner world.

'But work couldn't keep you away from this one, eh, Wolfe?'

The Director deigned not to reply.

Undeterred, Doug continued, 'The event should be quite something, hm?'

Steiner regarded him with eyes so brown they seemed black. A ribbed cupola braced his skull and held his head at a quizzical angle. His response came after a lapse of seconds.

'I cannot honestly say that I am anticipating the event.'

Doug rubbed his hands together, gave a quick wink to Abe. 'Oh, and why's that, Wolfe?'

The Director considered. 'In my opinion, tonight's event seems too calculated a response to be considered true art. Also, I am not sure that Tamara has recovered sufficiently from, and fully assimilated, her tragedy to produce a significant work on the subject.' He became silent. Points of light sequenced along the surface of the cupola below his right ear.

Perhaps to deter Doug's further jibes, Abe said, 'Won't this be your last social event on Meridian, Director? I've heard you're leaving.'

'I leave in less than a week,' Steiner replied. 'I might just make Tamara's next event. The date of embarkation has been put back due to unforeseen circumstances— '

'And what of Tamara,' Doug cut in, 'will she be going with you?'

Steiner seemed not to notice, or chose to ignore, Doug's provocations. 'I have asked Tamara to accompany me to my new posting.'

'And has she accepted?'

'That remains to be seen,' Steiner replied evenly.

Abe exchanged a glance with me. I knew that he felt as uneasy a spectator of this verbal duel as I did. He said, 'Perhaps you could tell me, Director – is there any truth to the rumour that the Telemass shots to Earth are to be reduced to one a month? I've heard there's been staff cuts at the station.'

I saw Doug glance at the Director, a slight smile on his lips, as if he knew something that we did not and was enjoying seeing Steiner cross-questioned.

'Earth–Meridian shots, and vice versa, will *not* be cut to one a month, Mr Cunningham,' Steiner said. 'Staff has been reduced, that is true. But this will in no way affect the regularity of imports and exports.'

'Is that so?' Doug asked. 'Then what's your "technical adviser" – isn't that how he was introduced? – doing here if everything is AOK?' He indicated the black-suited, bearded man Steiner had been talking to earlier.

'Weller's visit here is merely routine,' Steiner replied.

'But you don't deny things are slowing down on Meridian?' Doug went on. 'Tourism has taken a tumble over the past year, the mining operations have pulled out . . .'

'I suggest,' Steiner said testily, 'that you interrogate the economists on Main about these purported facts. I run the Telemass station, Inspector, not the planet.'

Doug sipped his drink, smiling to himself.

Steiner said, 'I received your message earlier, Mr Cunningham.' He turned to Doug. 'I presume you wanted to see me about this matter, Inspector?'

Doug nodded. 'Could you tell me if any of your technicians are missing, Wolfe?' he asked. 'The remains found today seem to belong to one of your men.'

Steiner lapsed into a trance. Lines of miniaturized text scrolled down his pupils. He came to and reported to the Inspector, 'I have five staff on furlough at the moment. They might be anywhere on Meridian.' He paused. 'Do you know how the technician died, Mr Cunningham?'

'Well, not really. It was obvious that a sand lion got to him at some point, but whether the animal was the cause of death . . .'

'Also,' Doug said, 'it's a bit of a mystery how the tech got out that far. There was no vehicle near by, or vehicle tracks, according to Abe and Bob. And he couldn't have walked so far out.'

'Is it possible that a lion might have attacked him near the coast and carried the remains inland?' Steiner asked.

Doug glanced at Abe, who shook his head. 'They're not known to venture anywhere near the coast. They live and hunt in an area one to two hundred kays into the interior. And they don't carry their victims. They devour them on the spot.'

Doug nodded. 'I might need to question you at some time. I'd be obliged if you could make yourselves available.'

There was a flurry of commotion behind us. Tamara Trevellion was making her way through an admiring throng of guests, the pretty girl and her surgeon in tow. Steiner excused himself, joined her and took her hand; he escorted the fish-woman towards our group, answering her questions on the way.

As I watched them, I wondered how the Director could bring himself to conduct an affair with a woman so alien.

We accommodated the artist into our circle. 'Mr Cunningham, Inspector Foulds.' She inclined her head to each in turn. 'Wolfe, my dear, do introduce me . . .' Her tone was imperious, without warmth. She stared down at me as I was introduced and extended a cold and bloodless hand. Barbels depended from her underslung jaw, their extremities illuminated like fibre optic cable.

'Delighted,' she said, far from convincingly.

Although Trevellion had retained her original form, it seemed as though she had been stretched, the bones and muscles of her limbs, and even those of her torso, drawn and attenuated to achieve some aesthetic at odds with any human criteria of beauty. Seen at a distance, she might have appeared strikingly slender and exotic; at close quarters, towering over Director Steiner and the rest of us, she struck me as a bizarre freak. When she took my hand I felt the cold sebaceous film that covered her body, and only then did I notice the parasitical sluglike fish that anchored themselves to her scales by suction and moved about her person with quick flips of their tails.

Now she laid four webbed fingers on Steiner's arm. 'I trust you have been keeping our guests entertained?' Her face was devoid of any expression I might have recognized, but I thought I detected a note of irony in her tone. The last thing that Director Steiner could be called upon to do was to 'entertain'.

'We were having a fascinating discussion,' Doug joined in the fun.

Steiner, augmented beyond such petty concerns, stood beside the fish-woman and took it all in silence – or perhaps he was lost in some abstraction known only to himself.

'I suppose he's been telling you about his treachery,' Trevellion went on.

At this, Steiner did respond. His eyes widened, as if the remark had jolted him. He stared at Trevellion.

'What treachery is this?' Doug asked, suppressing a smile.

'Oh, he didn't tell you?' She squeezed her lover's arm. 'Wolfe is deserting me.'

'That is hardly fair,' Steiner said. 'I have asked you to accompany me to my next posting, Tamara.'

'Will you go, Mrs Trevellion?' Doug asked.

'Meridian is my home now. I adore the place. I will never leave, no matter what.' At this she stared at Steiner, her flat grey eyes expressionless.

She changed the subject, addressing Abe. 'Mr Cunningham – Wolfe mentioned that you were discussing sand lions. Apparently you saw someone savaged on Brightside today?'

I drew a sharp breath and almost choked on my drink. I was unable to tell if Tamara Trevellion's reference to Brightside was intentional, another cruel jibe, or merely a *faux pas* of thoughtless insensitivity.

In the fraught silence that followed, I noticed the girl – Trevellion's maid or assistant, standing behind the fish-woman. She clearly wanted to say something, change the subject, but could not find the words to do so. She wore a wincing expression between pain and embarrassment.

Abe nodded. 'That's right,' he said. His stare was a challenge.

'Sand lions fascinate me,' Trevellion went on. 'They are the most ferocious animal native to the planet, are they not?'

Abe swirled his drink. 'You're well informed.'

'Do you know something,' she said, seemingly addressing us all, 'I rather think I would like one as a pet—'

'That's quite impossible,' Abe said, almost losing his cool.

'It is? But surely a lion could be operated upon so that it obeyed my commands?' She turned and gestured imperiously to her surgeon.

31

'Hathaway, what do you think?' The surgeon almost bowed, then whispered that such an operation was feasible.

I wanted suddenly to be elsewhere, away from the tableau of Trevellion's holding court, trampling over people's sensibilities with her thoughtless egotism.

The same thought had obviously occurred to the girl. She edged in beside me, pursed her lips tight and raised her eyes, as if to say: 'Here she goes again!' It was a relief to see features so animated after Trevellion's lugubrious expression.

The girl was small, with long fair hair, dark eyebrows and a pale, oval face. Her lips were so full they seemed swollen, giving her face a martyred look. I could not help but notice the threadbare state of the primrose dress that covered her thin body: she had about her the same unkempt and unsophisticated appearance as those who have ceased to look after themselves, like psychiatric patients. To complete her aspect of destitution, she was barefoot.

'How the hell can you stand the woman?' I asked.

She pursed her lips in a twisted, off-centre expression of resignation, shrugged stoically.

I said, 'I know, somebody has to do the dirty work . . .'

This time she smiled, then hesitated on the verge of saying something. 'Are you Mr Benedict,' she whispered at last, 'the pilot?' She glanced nervously at Trevellion, but the fish-woman was absorbed in conversation with her surgeon. 'I heard you announced.'

I was surprised that she had remembered. 'Ex-pilot,' I corrected her.

'You're the first pilot – *ex*-pilot – I've ever met,' she said shyly, avoiding my eyes. 'Were you on in-system runs?'

I nodded, wanting to steer the conversation away from this subject. 'Earth–Mars, most of the time.' I too had adopted a whisper, as if loath to interrupt Trevellion's monologue: she was now declaiming out loud the aesthetics of having a tamed lion on the island.

'But why did you leave? Why did you come here, of all places?'

I wondered, for a second, if I was being set up – but decided against it. The girl was too nervous, too shy, to be intentionally probing for the errors of my past.

'I'd had enough of piloting,' I answered. 'I wanted a quiet life. Meridian seemed just the planet.'

She shrugged, smiled. 'I know it's silly, but I've dreamed for years of escaping Meridian. I *hate* the place. I want nothing more than to get away.'

I laughed. 'Then why don't you?'

'Oh, that's impossible!' She said this with venom, then stopped suddenly as she became aware of the silence around us.

Tamara Trevellion had paused in her speech and was staring at the girl, who seemed to shrink into herself beside me. Never have I seen such a look of dismay on a face as I did then.

'You *know*,' Trevellion said, with an iciness entirely in keeping with her appearance, 'that I will not tolerate being interrupted. Perhaps you would like to enlighten us with your comment?'

'N-no,' the girl stammered. 'I . . . I'm, sorry—'

'In that case, I assume that you have something better to do with yourself than make a public exhibition of your ill manners?'

The girl looked stricken, hardly able to nod in cowed agreement. As she hurried away she glanced at me, and I saw the expression of wretchedness on her face. A tension had developed among the group, as if each one of us felt uneasy with ourselves for tolerating such arrogance.

I watched the girl run across the lawn and disappear into the dome.

'Well, Mr Cunningham,' Trevellion was saying, 'will you capture me a lion? I'll make sure that you are amply rewarded.'

'No matter what the reward, the answer is no. Brightside hold unpleasant memories for me. I don't want to risk my life just to satisfy a whim.'

Trevellion gestured. 'My offer is one hundred thousand credits. Please take your time and think it over.'

Before Abe could reply, Trevellion glanced at her scaled wrist and announced that it was time for the commencement of the event. She turned and swept from our circle, her fins rippling in the warm night air as she hurried across the garden.

Abe and I hung back, then followed the rest of the guests down a paved incline between scented bougainvillaea and the massive trumpet blooms of a native shrub. We passed over a stone bridge and came to the saddle-shaped greensward. Cushions littered the grass and the guests made themselves comfortable. Trays loaded with drinks floated through the gathering, and euphor-fumes snaked through the air. I was feeling far from euphoric.

'What a bitch,' I said, as we stretched out on foam-forms set into the bank of the hollow.

'Do you know something, Bob? I think she had absolutely no idea what she was asking me to do. She wanted a sand lion, and that's all she was thinking about.'

I was actually referring to Trevellion's treatment of the girl, but said nothing.

As we waited for the performance to begin, I thought of the girl and wished now that I had gone after her and said something, rather than allowed myself to be lured meekly to watch one of Tamara Trevellion's self-aggrandizing events. I was determined not to be impressed by what was to follow.

A hush settled over the audience. I looked around the hollow; I could not see Trevellion, but Wolfe Steiner was seated on the ground ten metres before us with a group of Augmenteds, staring up into the night sky. The lights, floating will-o'-the-wisps on the periphery of the hollow, dimmed one by one until absolute darkness descended.

The first floating screen, until now a dark oval the size of a flier blotting out the stars of Darkside, activated; its frame of separate neon strips ignited in sequence and created a flicker effect, bathing the audience in a wash of bright electric-blue light. Then with a startling crash of chords from a hidden speaker the screen suddenly expanded to fill half the sky above the hollow, and the guests below cried out first in alarm and then appreciation, and stared up in wonder. On the convex membrane of the screen, so vast I had to lie back to take in all of it, the first image resolved itself.

The scene was Earth, the Saharan artists' colony of Sapphire Oasis, and the subject was the crystal artist Max Trevellion at a party thrown to celebrate his engagement to Tamara Christiansen. The film was stock vid-footage, but subtly altered, computer enhanced. An accompanying voice-over spoke Tamara's early love poems. I had seen sufficient news-vids of Max Trevellion to know that the images of him here, sun-bathing beside a pool, working on a crystal, were idealized; skilfully, Tamara had altered the planes of his face, brightened his eyes, increased his height, and made his movements fluid and commanding. He seemed even to emanate a charismatic aura. Only when I heard the line: 'We apprehend our loved ones / With eyes of perfection . . .' did I realize that this image of him was not an improved version of Max Trevellion designed to make him something that he was not, but how Tamara Christiansen had actually seen her husband-to-be.

For the next thirty minutes we watched an historical account of the following twenty years: their wedding on Earth, their artistic collaborations, their move to Meridian. Tamara Trevellion appeared in all these as a tall, severe figure, handsome, perhaps striking – but not at all the Nordic Goddess she had been before her alterations. She had applied the same techniques of dissimulation to the portrayal of herself as she had to her husband, though in her case she presented her younger self in a cold, self-critical light.

Then the film concentrated on their individual artistic careers: Max went from strength to strength, attaining distinction with a series of crystals depicting life on Meridian, now exhibited in all the major galleries on Earth. For her part, Tamara seemed always to be in her husband's shadow. She seemed reluctant to exhibit her work, and the few pieces she did show gained only lukewarm response. Her poetry received popular acclaim, but Tamara despised this. It was as if the popularity of her verse served only to point up her lack of success in other artistic media.

The last scene of this first section of the event showed Max and Tamara working together on a crystal, with the voice-over: 'In creation / Our love combined, creating.'

The giant screen dimmed, plunging the hollow into darkness. There was a polite scatter of applause. As a resumé of their time together, and of Trevellion's view of herself and her husband, it had been entertaining enough. It set the scene for the tragedy to come, but could not in itself be called art. Max Trevellion came over as a genuinely warm and talented artist, and I began to feel sympathetic towards the man, began to feel the tragedy of his loss. Trevellion, for her part, had characterized herself as a nervous, self-doubting paranoid. More than once she had shown herself dissatisfied with her creations: one scene had her smashing to pieces a crystal she considered second-rate. I had always thought that there were two attitudes an artist can take to their work: they can egotistically assume that it is better than it actually is, or they can tell themselves that it could be better. Tamara Trevellion took the latter course to an extreme.

Then the second floating screen, redundant until now, activated its sequencing neon frame and expanded in a sudden, dizzying rush. Now the entirety of the heavens above us, the whole of our field of vision, was taken up by the over-reaching screens. A voice-over announced the date: a year ago today. The day, I realized, of the Telemass accident. An identical still image appeared on each screen; a photo-portrait of Max Trevellion, the two faces staring at each other from the convex hemispheres. Then the image to our left unfroze and the show resumed.

For the next hour, each screen played alternately. The first, for the next five minutes, presented a factual account of what had happened during a period of a few hours on that fateful day. Then that image froze and the facing screen showed what I could only assume was an idealized version of the events, how Trevellion *wanted* the day to have progressed.

Fate is inevitable, she seemed to be saying, tragedy requires a victim: therefore, take *this* victim . . .

On the left screen, we watched Max Trevellion report that his daughter was ill: he would make the trip to Earth in her place. The audience watched, spellbound. I felt something catch in my throat with the realization that, with these words, Trevellion had consigned himself to oblivion. Then, on the right screen, we watched a small, fair-haired girl ready herself excitedly for her trip to Earth.

At the sight of her I sat forward, my heart thumping.

'The girl . . .' I whispered to Abe.

He glanced at me. 'Of course, didn't you know? She's Trevellion's daughter, Fire.'

'She is? But I thought . . .'

I returned my attention to the right screen, appalled and fascinated. The girl going through the motions that would, in Tamara Trevellion's revisionist version of events, lead to her death was the same girl who, one hour earlier, Trevellion had treated with absolute contempt. The girl I had assumed was her maid or companion was in fact her daughter . . .

As I watched, I saw that Trevellion had employed the same technique to subtly alter her daughter's appearance as she had to enhance her husband's.

Fire Trevellion was, in reality, very attractive; in this version, her features had been taken and shifted slightly, skewed, so that while still recognizably Fire's, the face had lost all its appeal, its character. She was not quite ugly in her mother's revised scenario, but she was made somehow . . . peevish, mean-spirited. I felt a slow anger welling at Trevellion's deceit. I wondered how many of the guests were aware of what she had done.

Then the show switched to the left screen, the screen which showed what had really happened, and we watched Tamara kiss her husband farewell, to a rousing fanfare and the lines: 'The tragedy of their parting / Was that they knew not the tragedy.' We watched Max Trevellion take his place on the Telemass pad beside the two other tachyon-passengers to Earth, watched him flash out of existence accompanied by a mighty crash of cymbals, then silence.

The right screen: Fire Trevellion said goodbye to her parents, who, arm in arm, very much in love, watched her take her place on the pad and disappear in a flash of white light. They turned, all smiles, and left the station. Voice-over: 'Fate takes, and though the tragedy is great / It can be overcome.' But I knew the lines to be sanctimonious platitudes, lies. Had Fire taken her father's place that fateful day, the tragedy for Tamara would not have been so great.

But the show was not yet over.

Trevellion had one more victim to sacrifice.

As we watched, the two screens merged, became one all-encompassing membrane like the inner surface of a dome. A blurred image emerged. I was shocked to see Director Wolfe Steiner, enthroned in his command chair in the Telemass Control Centre – but not the Wolfe Steiner as we knew him. Trevellion's graphics had taken his aloofness, his coldness, his augmentation and emphasized all three, so that now he resembled nothing more than a caricature of his former self, a heartless, inhuman calculating machine. She had employed monotone graphics, hard angles to achieve the effect. As with Fire, she had remoulded his features: she had made him less human, more a sharp-featured adjunct of his augmentation.

We were swamped by the magnified image of Steiner, giving orders to his technicians as they attempted to retrieve the vector along which

Max Trevellion and the others were lost. He was portrayed doing this with no display of emotion whatever, which, as Trevellion intended, had the effect of creating an atmosphere of hostility among the audience – but would passion on his part have done anything more to save the artist? Then we watched him break the news to the families, again with total impassivity. We watched him face the inquest, answer questions, accept the verdict of not guilty with all the emotion of an android. We were manipulated into feeling hatred towards Wolfe Steiner, and when the lines rolled out: 'They found him free from blame / But would *they* have found him guilty?' I think that the majority of the audience was on Trevellion's side in her detestation of the Director. I saw a tall figure hurry past where we were seated and leave the hollow, and when I looked to where I'd seen Wolfe Steiner earlier, his foam-form was empty.

I recalled Doug Fould's opinion that their liaison was suspicious, and I knew now that he was right: Steiner had been set up. I thought I understood Trevellion's grief at her loss, but I could not begin to understand why, instead of trying to heal herself, perhaps learn from grief and create from it as artists should, she had vindictively hit out and unjustly slighted both Steiner and her daughter.

I rose and strode quickly from the hollow. As the giant frozen image of Steiner's caricatured face faded from the screen, cloaking my retreat in welcome darkness, I was amazed to hear the beginnings of applause behind me, then louder as the audience gave their full support to Trevellion's twisted catalogue of spite. I needed to get away, to be alone for a time. It was as if the greensward was contaminated by Trevellion's inhumanity, as if by remaining there I might tacitly condone her creation.

I hurried from the gathering and found myself on a cliff-top path overlooking a deserted beach. I followed it down to the sheltered cove, then walked along the firm stretch of sand beside the ocean. The only illumination was from the massed stars above Darkside.

In the gloom before me I heard a small sound of surprise, then, 'Mr Benedict?'

I peered. 'Fire?'

She quickly backhanded what might have been a tear from her cheek. She perched on a rock, her knees drawn up to her chin. She smiled as I approached. 'I thought it was you, Mr Benedict.'

I sat beside her. In the cold light of the stars she seemed reduced in size and substance, a two-dimensional silver engraving. On her left knee I made out the sheen of saliva and the imprint of teeth.

I gestured towards the hilltop. 'Listen,' I began, 'I'm sorry.'

She looked away. 'Forget it.'

'I wanted to say something to your mother, tell her what I felt.'

'What could you have said?' Her tone was hopeless.

'Perhaps I might have made her see how rude she was . . .'

Fire turned large green eyes on me, curiously innocent beneath the high fringe. 'You're talking about earlier, when Tamara got mad at me for interrupting?'

'Of course.'

She laughed. 'I'm not bothered about that! She treats me like that all the time. Of course, in front of strangers . . .' She shrugged with a kind of determined resolve. 'I can handle it.'

'You mean . . . ?' I gestured. 'You saw your mother's show?' I had hoped that she might have been spared witnessing the event.

Without meeting my gaze, she nodded. 'I sneaked out of my room. Pretty cruel, wasn't it?' She went on, with a forced gaiety which I guessed belied her true feelings, 'Did you see how she portrayed me, Mr Benedict? I've known all along that she would rather I'd gone instead of my father – I can live with that. But to portray me as ugly as she did . . . there was no reason for that.'

'I'm sorry,' I said, inadequately.

She stared out at the waves, silver crested in the starlight. 'And in front of all those people,' she said almost wistfully. 'That was the worst thing of all. I can put up with her hatred in private – but in public like that it just makes both of us look small.'

I wondered then if she had heard the applause.

A silence came between us. I was suddenly afraid that she might regret sharing her pain with a perfect stranger and decide to leave, so I said the first thing that came into my head.

'How old are you, Fire?'

She had to think about it. 'Nineteen standard.'

I shrugged. 'So what's keeping you here? Why don't you get out, if you don't like the way your mother's treating you?'

'Is that an offer, Mr Benedict? Shall we elope? We could go to Earth. I'd like nothing more.'

I smiled. 'I can't see why you don't just pack your bags and move to another island.'

'Listen, I know you mean well, but you don't know the half of it. I'm sick and I need my treatment and it's expensive and only Tamara can afford it, OK? If it wasn't for Tamara and Fats up there, I'd be dead.'

'I had no idea . . . I'm sorry.'

She turned on me. 'Hey, don't you think I want to escape? I'm sometimes tempted to leave and to hell with the consequences. I often think a month or two of freedom, away from Tamara, would be worth dying for. But I always chicken out, stay here and take the abuse.'

I attempted to lighten the tone of the conversation. 'What do you do here? Do you work?'

She sighed. 'I run after Tamara. I'm her secretary, housemaid, cook. I make sure she has all the right materials to hand. I've done all this since I was ten.'

'Can't you get out a bit, explore the islands?'

She seemed to shrink into herself. 'Tamara wouldn't like that,' she said in a small voice.

I wanted to tell her, to hell with what Tamara would or wouldn't like. Then I reminded myself that she had had almost twenty years of this conditioning, was subservient beyond the point where mere verbal coaxing would stir thoughts of rebellion.

I was aware that she was looking at me.

I was shocked by what she said next.

'How long have you been taking frost, Mr Benedict?'

I stared at her. 'How do you know—?'

She smiled. 'Tamara was dependent, once. I recognize the signs. Pale skin, the eyes. You look like you take a lot.'

I was momentarily nonplussed. I had discussed my use of the drug with no one before now. 'A little,' I said.

'Are you hooked?'

I hesitated. 'Habituated, let's say. I could stop tomorrow.'

'That's what Tamara said—'

'Then how did she get off it?'

'Her surgeon weaned her off. Then he Altered her. She doesn't need the stuff now. Her metabolism manufactures a different drug which gives her a safer, permanent high.'

She paused, then said, 'Who supplies you, Mr Benedict?'

'No one. I gather it and prepare it myself.'

'From Brightside?' There was surprise in her tone.

'It grows wild out there,' I began.

'So . . . you get lots of the stuff?'

I shrugged, uneasy at her questions. 'A fair amount.'

She was watching me closely. 'Mr Benedict . . . I don't suppose you'd consider getting me some frost, would you?'

'I don't know . . .'

'Why not? You said I ought to get away from here. I can't do it physically, so what's wrong with the alternative? We could meet here, same time tomorrow. You could stay with me while I take it, make sure I do nothing stupid. I'd pay you for it.'

'I don't want paying.'

'Then you'll bring me some?' Her smile, at the thought of it, won me over.

'Just enough for one trip,' I told her, wondering what I was getting myself into. 'No more.'

'Great! Moor your launch in the next cove, Mr Benedict. It can't be seen from the dome.'

She started suddenly at a sound from along the beach. 'Shhh! I think it's Tamara.'

I smiled. I wanted to tell her that she was being paranoid.

'If she found me down here, talking to you, when I should be in my room . . .' Her face in the starlight wore a mask of fright.

'I must go, Mr Benedict!'

I had expected her to take the cliff path, but instead she dashed to the undergrowth at the foot of the cliff. I followed her. She had parted the fronds of a fern and was squirming into a narrow gap between two rocks.

'Fire . . . ?'

She turned her head awkwardly. 'It's a tunnel I found,' she panted. 'It leads up to the garden outside my room. It's the only secret I have from Tamara. I'll see you tomorrow!' And with that she was gone.

I left the beach, passing as I did so not Trevellion, as Fire had feared, but a couple of Augmented lovers, strolling in the starlight. I took the path to the top of the cliff and rejoined the party on the illuminated lawn, considering Fire Trevellion and her situation.

I had no wish to make the acquaintance of Tamara Trevellion again tonight, and when I located Abe I was relieved when he suggested that we leave.

'Where've you been, Bob? I've been ready to go since that so-called event. Tamara's been obnoxious. She seems to think she's created something of lasting importance. And what's all the more sickening, her sycophants tend to agree.'

Back at my dome in the early hours, I sat on the patio and thought through the events of the evening, the screen-show and my meeting with Trevellion's daughter. Then I found the frost flowers where I'd flung them that afternoon and set about preparing the drug. I made a dilute solution for Fire tomorrow, filled the half-shell for my immediate use and stashed away the remainder.

I returned to the patio with a small dose in the burner to see me through the night. I thought about reliving my meeting with Fire, but decided against it. It was too recent in my mind, and surrounded by too many ugly incidents – the discovery of the technician's remains, the night's event, the way Trevellion had treated her daughter. If any of these intruded while I concentrated on my time with Fire, I risked subjecting myself to the nightmare of a bad trip. Instead, I thought of that holiday twenty years ago, the beach and the slim blonde girl, not at all unlike Fire Trevellion. I applied a light to the sparkling pink powder and it ignited with a hiss, giving off thick, acrid fumes.

I inhaled deeply, and dreamed.

3

JADE

I was awoken the following afternoon by some insistent but indefinable sound working at the edge of my consciousness.

For perhaps thirty seconds after coming to my senses, all I could recall was the dream I had lived through during the night. I remembered the sand and the sunlight, the taste of feta and olives, the sound of cicadas chirruping and a girl laughing. It was as if no time at all had elapsed since the idyll of my youth, as if I had awoken from a drunken sleep and could return to the beach merely by stepping from the dome. Then I recalled the reality to which the dome belonged, and I was suddenly overwhelmed by the fact of who and where I was. Recollection of the accident descended like a sudden migraine. I took frost to banish the nightmares and to give me a period of forgetting, but always upon awakening the remembering was intensified.

I was in the lounge. At some point, perhaps when the effect of the frost had worn off and exhaustion took over, I must have dragged myself from the patio and collapsed on the chesterfield, but I had no recollection of doing so. I forced myself into a sitting position and groaned. My initial thought was that I should take refuge in another frost-induced escape, but I knew that a second dose, so soon after the first, would not prove as effective – and anyway I was due to meet Fire Trevellion that evening.

I sat and stared through the clear wall of the dome at the flickering aurora of Brightside, contemplating the move I should make to take a shower and fix a meal. I managed to convince myself that there was no hurry. I might have been asleep for most of the day, but there was still plenty of time before the fall of darkness and the rendezvous. I lay back and closed my eyes, and only then did I become fully aware of the noise which had awoken me.

I stepped from the lounge on to the patio and stared down at the brilliant blue sea. The wake of a hover-scooter scored a direct white slash across the surface of the ocean, mirroring the con-trail of a jet overhead. As I watched, the vehicle hit the island and negotiated the winding path up to my dome.

Doug lowered his scooter to the ground beyond the patio, removed his helmet, and strolled over. Unlike last night, today he wore his navy-blue uniform and jackboots, and unlike last night, when the euphor-fumes had made him genial, he was grave. His face was bright red from over-exposure to the sun.

'Doug, can I get you a drink?'

'I could do with a long, cool juice. I've been Brightside all day. That's what I came to see you about.'

I fixed two juices from the dispenser and carried them across the patio to a foam-form overlooking the sea. 'Have you found out who the tech was?' I asked.

He leaned against the balcony rail. 'Well, as a matter of fact we haven't. That's going to be a little difficult. You see, we didn't find the remains.'

'You did know where to look?'

'Abe gave me the co-ordinates last night. We searched the whole area. I still have three men out there. We found where the cage was set down, and the displaced sand from Abe's launch. But no bones—'

'But there had to be something there. What about disturbed ground, tracks?'

'Nothing. There were no tracks, no signs of any disturbance. The area was clean.'

'Maybe some scavenger made off with the remains?'

'Fine. But where are the tracks?'

I shrugged. 'A strong wind could have obliterated them.'

'And left the imprint of Abe's cage, and all your footprints, a hundred metres away, completely undisturbed? Bob, are you absolutely sure that you saw a body out there?'

'Doug, we saw the damned thing being torn to pieces—'

'Brightside can do strange things to the mind,' Doug said, 'play tricks with a man's vision . . .'

'If you doubt what we saw, Abe has all the evidence you need.' I told him about the scrap of uniform bearing the Telemass logo.

He remained unconvinced. 'I know about that. Abe told me all about it when I contacted him an hour ago. Thing is, it's quite conceivable that you found that out there and nothing else. The rest could have been . . . I don't know – a mirage. Stranger things have happened.'

I shook my head. 'I know what I saw.'

'Then how do you explain the total absence of *anything* out there now?'

I avoided his stare and gestured lamely.

'I have someone checking the whereabouts of every Telemass technician on Meridian,' he went on. 'If they're all present and accounted for, then as far as I'm concerned the case is closed.'

'I see your point. But what about the remains of the uniform we found? How did that get out there?'

He shrugged, uninterested. 'Search me, Bob. Does it matter? If we can't find a body, and it turns out that no one's missing . . .'

'I suppose that's fair enough.' I indicated his empty glass. 'How about another drink?'

I fixed two more juices.

'What did you think of the party last night?' he asked when I returned.

'Well . . . the actual event was one of the most shallow and spiteful things I've ever witnessed.'

He nodded. 'I have to agree. Didn't I tell you that there was something odd about Trevellion taking Steiner as her lover? But I must admit, I never expected that to happen. I didn't think Trevellion could sink so low. Did you stay to the end?'

'We left about an hour after the event.'

'Then you missed the confrontation between Trevellion and Steiner?'

'I'm not sure I want to hear about it.'

'Steiner didn't leave the island after stalking from the performance area. A couple of hours later he returned to the garden and found Trevellion. She was holding forth to a group of admirers, explaining

45

some involved metaphor of the bloody event. Anyway, Steiner accused her of slander, defamation of character. I could see that he was angry, even though he handled himself with dignity. It was the first time I'd seen him remotely moved.'

'What happened?'

'Well, they didn't quite come to blows. Steiner said he was thinking of prosecuting Trevellion, and she replied that he wouldn't dare. It sounded like a threat—'

I stopped him. 'Just like that – "You wouldn't dare"? As if she might have something on him?'

Doug shrugged. 'I don't know. Maybe – something he doesn't want making public? Anyway, at this Steiner just shut up and strode off. I must admit, I don't much care for him, but he had my sympathies yesterday.'

'It was pretty obvious that you two don't get on.'

He smiled. 'We've had our differences in the past,' he said. 'The last being on the subject of the Telemass scaledown.'

'I thought that was just a rumour?'

He looked up from his drink. 'It's official policy, Bob. The authorities on Meridian have been told, but Steiner hasn't made it public yet. I suggested that he should, and he more or less told me to mind my own business. I think he's biding his time until he leaves, and then he'll leave the dirty work of making the thing public to his successor. Steiner is, in essence, a very weak man. He's a puppet of his commanders on Earth.'

'I thought you were rather hard on him last night,' I said. 'How drastic is the scaledown?'

'The shots'll be reduced to one a month, each way. Meridian has been designated a backwater world.'

I thought about it. 'Could Trevellion have known about this? Perhaps she was threatening she'd make it public if Steiner prosecuted for slander?'

'I don't think so. It has to come out sooner or later, it's just a matter of who'll make the announcement.'

I considered my drink. 'How well do you know Tamara Trevellion?' I asked.

'Not very well at all, Bob. She's a very private person, even more so since the death of her husband. After last night, I'm beginning to think that the loss affected her more than it seemed at the time.'

'I don't suppose you know her daughter?' I asked casually.

'Fire?' He shook his head. 'Can't say I've really taken much notice of her. She's a nervous wreck and she's scared stiff of her mother. Trevellion treats her like dirt. After last night's performance it's pretty obvious why.'

'Someone told me that Fire's ill,' I said.

'First I've heard about it.'

'Apparently that's why she remains on the island. She's receiving treatment from Trevellion's surgeon and can't do without it.'

'Poor wretch! She really should leave the island. The place must hold terrible memories for her.'

I looked at him. 'Why? What happened?'

'You haven't heard about it?' He sounded surprised. 'Fire had a sister, Jade, a few years her elder. Five years ago she was killed in an accident on the island. Apparently, Fire saw it happen. I don't know the full details. I was only a sergeant then. My superior handled the affair. But I do know that Fire was in trauma for a long time.'

'My God, the poor kid.'

'The family's had more than its fair share of bad luck. No wonder Tamara's such an unlikeable person, she's the product of one tragedy after another.'

Doug looked at his watch. He finished his drink. 'I really must be getting off, Bob. I want to call in on Abe before dark. Hey – and how about we get some gliding in soon?'

I murmured something in agreement and Doug ambled over to his machine. I watched him replace his helmet, mount the scooter, and set off down the hillside. When he hit the sea, he accelerated from the bay in the direction of Abe's island.

I remained on the patio until the shield appeared in the distance, presaging the fall of night. Over Darkside, the stars slowly brightened in the darkness of deep space, but tonight the sight left me curiously untroubled.

I returned to the lounge, sat down and considered the sachet of frost I had prepared for Fire.

One hour later, as twilight descended, I cast off from the jetty and steered the launch out across the open sea towards Trevellion's island.

The crossing was calm. At this time in the evening, with the leaning edge of the orbital shield rapidly shutting out the sunlight, the sea had the peculiar property of being lighter than the sky as it reflected the aurora of Brightside. As the darkness deepened, the ocean took on the colour of blood. Thirty minutes after setting out, I manoeuvred the launch around Trevellion's island, a dark wedge of land studded with the occasional laser sculpture and *objet d'art* scintillating in the dying light. On the summit of the island, Trevellion's dome glowed like a diamond. The thought that she might have seen my arrival, and so would not allow Fire to meet me, created a hard knot of apprehension in my chest.

I steered into the cove, which Fire had pointed out last night, and moored the launch to a tumbledown pier. A sandy footpath rounded the headland to the bay where we had arranged to meet.

I followed the path and paused when I came to the beach. In the light of the stars I made out the small figure of Fire Trevellion. She was strolling along the margin of wet sand beside the sea, with a negligence born of either boredom or dejection. She wore a pair of shorts and a halter top, and she carried a thin computer board. From time to time she paused, allowing the incoming waves to foam around her ankles, consulted the glowing screen and then continued strolling, addressing words to the ocean.

I walked across the sand and followed her footsteps. Fire paused again, but this time tossed the computer board up the beach as if she had had quite enough of that for one night. She stared out to sea, her hands pocketed behind her. As I approached, she turned suddenly without moving her legs, and the torque of her torso was at once awkward and becoming. Her smile was genuine. 'Mr Benedict, I thought you'd never get here.'

I was, perhaps, ten minutes late – but I was realistic enough to realize that her pleasure at seeing me had more to do with the promise of frost than anything else.

I indicated the computer board, projecting from the sand like a headstone. 'What were you reciting?'

'Nothing interesting. Only poetry.' She smiled. 'I'm glad you came.'

Her long hair was gathered and tied in a pony-tail. I noticed that the pink material of her halter top and shorts had the worn, second-hand look of hand-me-downs, and I wondered if they had once belonged to her mother, before her alteration.

As if uneasy under my scrutiny, she looked away, up the hillside, to where the apex of the lighted dome could just be seen. She took my arm in a surprisingly strong grip. 'Come on. If Tamara comes out she'll see us. Can you imagine what she might say . . . ?' We hurried across the beach to a path which continued around the island.

'My mother likes only invited guests to visit. She even has security men guarding the island. It's OK, though,' she reassured me, 'they're patrolling the marina tonight. I hope you aren't angry with me for putting you in this situation?'

I laughed. 'Of course I'm not. I'm glad to be here.'

I could tell that Fire was nervous. Her chatter was an attempt to disguise the fact. 'If Tamara asks me where I've been when I get in, I'll . . . I'll say that I needed a long walk to learn the lines. I can recite most of them off by heart already, so she can't complain.'

Not for the first time I wanted to tell her to forget her mother.

Once out of sight of the dome, we slowed and strolled along the cliff-top path. Fire said, 'If I remember rightly, I did all the talking yesterday. Now it's your turn. I asked Tamara about you today. She knows all about everyone on Meridian. She told me that you came here after a smallship accident. Is that right?'

'How much did she tell you?'

She seemed to flinch at my tone. Her smile faltered. 'Only that much. She said you'd survived an accident, then retired. That's all.'

'I'm sorry. It's something I don't usually talk about.' I shrugged. 'That's about all there is to tell. I survived a freak accident and decided to get out. You don't often survive accidents like that. I was lucky. I didn't want to push that luck.'

I prayed, then, that she would not ask me why I took frost. I had lied to her once today and did not want to do so again. She was so ingenuous and credulous that to lie to her was like committing physical violence.

We sat on a bench overlooking the sea, watching as a flight of

49

pterosaurs made for Brightside. A warm breeze lapped around the island.

'Did you bring the frost?' she asked in a small voice.

I answered her with a question of my own. 'Why do you need it, Fire?'

She frowned at me. Her blonde fringe made her look very young. 'Like I told you yesterday – I want to escape.'

'You've had a hell of a past. What do you want to remember?'

She looked hurt. 'Oh, there were some good times, too,' she reassured me. 'It wasn't all bad.' She regarded me, her smile fixed with apprehension lest I deny her the drug I had promised.

'Look,' I said, avoiding her eyes, 'I know about Jade.'

She flashed me a look. 'How did you find out? Who told you?'

'Doug Foulds happened to mention it earlier today.'

She turned away, shrugged her shoulders. 'So . . . What about it?'

'So, it was the most traumatic event in your past. It'd be dangerous to relive a time when Jade was alive. You might easily find yourself reliving the tragedy by mistake—'

She just looked at me, with an earnestness I found disconcerting. 'But that's exactly what I want to do, Mr Benedict! I want to live through the accident again.'

I stared at her, hardly able to believe that someone so innocent might harbour such macabre desires. 'The trauma would be more than you could take. Do you realize that it's not just like a vivid memory? You'd actually *be* there, experiencing the reality of the accident.' I stared at her, shook my head. 'Why on earth would you want to put yourself through that all over again?'

She remained silent for a while, staring at her fingers. She looked up. 'I know it might seem strange to you, Mr Benedict. But, you see, I have no memory of the accident.' She glanced at me, a look of pleading in her eyes. 'The incident is one big blank, a gap. I don't think you understand what it's like. I loved Jade; she was the only person ever to show me any affection. And then she was gone. I want to know the truth of what happened. However terrible her death was, it can't be as bad as the nightmares I've had about it.'

'If you relive the accident through frost, you might not be able to stand the shock. Why do you think you blanked it out in the first place?'

She pushed both hands through her hair in a desperate gesture and left them there. 'I don't know! Maybe I couldn't handle it then. But it isn't safe to keep things repressed. I'm stronger now. I need to know.'

She drew her knees to her chest and hugged her legs, her eyes closed. I wanted to make some gesture of sympathy or affection, but found myself unable to do so.

'Have you ever spoken about the accident to anyone?' I asked.

She shook her head. She had opened her eyes and was staring out to sea. 'How could I? I can't remember anything.'

'Perhaps it might be safer if you talked about Jade with me – that might unlock memories.' I hesitated. 'Have you any idea where the accident happened?'

She remained silent for a long time, staring stubbornly straight ahead. 'I don't know. That is, I'm not sure. I *think* I know, but I've never been told. It's just a feeling I have.'

'Perhaps if we went there . . . ?' I suggested.

She looked at me. 'Do you think it might help?'

'It might. If you feel up to it, that is.'

'I don't know. I haven't been there in years. It frightens me.'

'The actual memory will be far more frightening, Fire.'

She shook her head, looking puzzled. 'You'd think so, wouldn't you? But the memory is somewhere in here, part of me, waiting to be unlocked and remembered. Where it happened, or where I think it happened – that's somehow more real, threatening . . .'

'It might be the first step towards remembering,' I said.

I stood, and after a moment's hesitation Fire joined me. We continued along the pathway which followed the outline of the island, the sea below to our right and a plantation of trees and shrubs to our left. Our way was illuminated by a series of small lights strung out on a cable along the length of the path. We came to a clearing, a sloping greensward stretching up to the hilltop. Fire halted and quickly grasped my hand like a child in need of reassurance.

'This is it, Mr Benedict.'

We stepped from the path and strolled up the hillside. The night phase was well upon us now, but the greensward was lighted by the stars over Darkside and the glow of the lights beside the path. The clearing was filled with the fragrance from the blooms in the

51

surrounding shrubbery. I found it hard to imagine that this pleasant glade could have been the venue for so tragic an event as the death of Fire's sister.

Then her hand tightened on mine and I could feel her shaking. 'I hate this place! Don't you feel it? The evil?'

'You can't recall anything?'

She shook her head. 'Nothing, not a thing. That's what's so frightening. Perhaps if I could remember something, then I wouldn't be so afraid. Does that make any sense?'

I walked her up the incline like an invalid. 'I know what you mean,' I said, not at all sure that I did.

'It's the absence of memory that makes this place so forbidding. Everywhere else on the island holds memories for me, except here. That's what makes me think this *must* be the place.' She glanced about her in silent desperation, her green eyes wide.

'Something else – Tamara never mentions this place. Sometimes she makes me accompany her on walks, but we never stop here. When we pass it on the path, she always hurries on.'

We had come to a halt in the centre of the glade.

From holding her hand, I thought it the natural thing to do to put a protective arm around her shoulders. 'Tell me about Jade,' I said.

I felt the slight movement of a shrug beneath my arm, as much to say that she did not want to talk.

'It can only help,' I prompted.

'Oh . . .' Something caught in her throat. 'I wouldn't know where to begin.'

'How old was she when the accident happened?'

Another shrug. 'About my age now, nineteen, twenty. I was fifteen. We were very much alike. We had our mother's looks, before she was altered, and our father's calm temperament. When I think back, I seem to recall that we were always together.'

'What kinds of things did you two get up to?'

Fire smiled. 'With Tamara and Max busy so much of the time, we were left to ourselves. We'd explore the forest – the "jungle" we called it – take a small boat around the coves. The usual stuff kids get up to. I remember one time . . .'

She went on, recounting the games and adventures of her child-hood. It seemed that, when talking of her sister, she recalled true happiness. She had said earlier that her sister was the only person ever to show her any real affection, and I was pained when I thought of what a loss her sister's death must have been.

For a time while she spoke, it seemed that she was quite unaware of where she was and who she was talking to. She paused, smiled at me. 'Do you know something, Mr Benedict? I feel closer to my sister than I have in years.'

At my urging, we continued up the slope.

'Did Tamara allow Jade off the island?' I asked.

She pushed a strand of sun-bleached hair from her face, reflectively. 'No . . . No, she didn't. You see, she had the same complaint as I have now. She needed constant treatment.'

I hesitated. 'What is your condition?' I asked.

'Oh' – she sounded casual, a little out of breath from the hike – 'I don't know its proper medical term, but I have a tumour in my cerebellum. It's actually inoperable, but my mother's surgeon can keep it in check with drugs.' She spoke casually, with an off-handedness which I thought might disguise her true despair.

'Is it painful?'

She frowned. 'No, not as such. I get the occasional headache. And sometimes I feel pretty washed out.' She smiled at me. 'But I can live with it.'

'Haven't you ever thought of seeking a second opinion?' I asked. 'If you could hire your own doctor you might be able to get away a bit.'

She looked away from me. 'Like I told you yesterday, the treatment's expensive, more creds than I could ever earn.'

I shrugged. 'Tamara could let you have your freedom, though, and still pay for your treatment.'

'I couldn't do that, Mr Benedict. Tamara needs me here.' She took my hand and hauled me the last few metres to the top of the hill.

We were standing before a large hexagonal plinth, similar to those that Trevellion used around the island to mount various works of art. This plinth was empty.

Fire was staring at the obsidian hexagon. 'Tamara and Jade were working on a piece when Jade died. Tamara completed it – I've heard that some experts think it her finest work.'

'What happened to it?'

'She sold it. It's housed on Main Island, in the Museum of Modern Art. I've never seen it.' She shivered. 'I've never really wanted to because it was the last thing Jade ever did – even if Tamara would let me. I don't know, perhaps I should go some day . . .'

Her sudden introspection made me uneasy. The glade had had the effect of subduing her. I began to wonder about the advisability of bringing her here. I held out my hand. 'Shall we move on?'

She remained standing beside the plinth, regarding me. 'Have you brought the frost, Mr Benedict?' she asked.

'Fire . . .' I began in exasperation.

She just stared at me, defiant. 'You said you would, Mr Benedict!'

I turned and started off down the hillside. Half-way towards the cliff-top path, I heard Fire running after me, her steps thumping breath from her lungs. She caught up with me and planted herself in my path, facing me and panting hard.

'Mr Benedict, I need to know how she died!'

'You wouldn't be able to take it, Fire. The knowledge all at once like that would be too much.'

'How do you know it would? You don't even know what happened!' Now she was walking backwards down the hill, almost shouting at me, pleading.

I stopped and held her by the shoulders. 'Listen, Fire – I could find out. When I know what happened, then I can decide whether it's safe for you to take the drug.'

'How can you find out?' she cried, and then in panic, 'Don't ask Tamara! If she found out that I wanted to know . . . She doesn't like me mentioning it.'

'I'm a friend of Doug Foulds. I can get him to find out what exactly happened.'

'And then you'll give me the frost?'

'Then I'll *tell* you what happened, see if that provokes any memories. You might be able to unlock the accident without resorting to the drug.'

'And if that doesn't work?'

'I don't know . . . Then we'd have to see where we stood.' I lowered my hands from her shoulders. 'Maybe then you can have the drug.'

She nodded, her expression tight as if she knew she had scored a minor victory. 'That seems fair enough.' She smiled and held out her hand. 'I'm sorry for shouting, Mr Benedict. A truce?'

With mock formality I took her hand and shook it.

Fire shivered. 'Come on, it's getting late. I told Tamara I'd be out for only an hour.'

We hurried along the cliff-top path to the beach where we had met and stood awkwardly in the sand preparatory to parting.

'Are you doing anything tomorrow, Bob?' she asked casually. It was the first time she had used my first name.

'Nothing much,' I said.

'You will contact Inspector Foulds?'

I nodded. 'I'll do that in the morning.'

She avoided my eyes. 'Then perhaps we could meet here tomorrow afternoon, around three—?'

She stopped suddenly. She was staring at something behind me, in the sea.

I turned and followed the direction of her transfixed gaze.

I made out the shape of a fin break the surface of the ocean, followed by the dark length of the creature's back. It was heading directly for the beach.

Fire gripped my arm in sudden fright.

'Hey,' I laughed, 'haven't you ever seen a big fish before?'

Only then did it come to me that the water this close to the shore would be too shallow for a fish of this size and, hard on this realization, the creature rose to its full height and emerged with a certain arrogant elegance from the swirling foam.

Fire quickly let go of my arm, as if scalded.

Tamara Trevellion strode from the ocean, her steps retarded by the drag of the undertow. Silver droplets cascaded from her streamlined limbs. Her scales winked iridescent in the starlight and a host of jet black parasites teemed about her body.

She halted before us.

Her face, at best emotionless, now seemed set in an expression of lugubrious disapproval, emphasized by her underhung jaw. She regarded us with large wet eyes rinsed by the ocean of the slightest charity.

Beside me, I was aware that Fire was frozen to the spot.

'Fire,' Trevellion said, 'I see that you have taken it upon yourself to invite strangers to my island. I hope for your sake that you have a suitable excuse.'

'I—'

Trevellion opened her gills and shunted air in what might have been a snort of anger. It had the immediate effect of silencing the girl.

Trevellion turned gelid eyes upon me. 'Ah . . . Benedict, isn't it? The ex-starship pilot.' Something in the way she pronounced my old profession suggested derision. I recalled that she had told Fire about my accident. I wondered how much she knew.

'Fire,' Trevellion addressed her daughter. 'To your room, immediately.'

Fire hurried off without so much as a murmur of protest.

'Benedict,' Trevellion said when we were alone. 'I must warn you that this island is off limits to all but a select few individuals whom *I* invite. There are many priceless works of art exhibited here.'

'I might be an unwitting trespasser' – I said the first thing that came into my head '– but I am not a thief. Fire invited me. I saw no reason not to accept. She is an adult—'

'For your information, Benedict, Fire is little more than a child. Her sickness has precluded her from experiencing the ways of the outside world. She has a rare neurological condition that requires constant and vigilant attention. That is why I apply the strictest conditions to my daughter's daily routine. Her health is my utmost priority.'

'Our talking did no harm.'

'One of the provisos of Fire's continued health is that she does not become excited.' She hesitated, regarding me with large flat eyes. 'I noticed you earlier in the glade. What did Fire want there?'

I shrugged, gaining time. 'She wanted nothing there. We merely went for a walk—'

'Did she mention her sister?'

I shook my head. 'No, she didn't.' I was conscious of my heartbeat, and hoped that Trevellion would not see through the lie.

'Good,' she said. 'The incident traumatized her, and she becomes depressed when she dwells on it.' She regarded me in silence, then said, 'Just what *did* you talk about, Benedict?'

I cleared my throat. 'That's between Fire and myself,' I said.

Trevellion stretched her lips in what might have been a smile. 'I presume she found time to ask you to take her away from here?'

Before I could find a reply, she went on, 'I might as well tell you, for your own good, that you are not the first. Fire uses her obvious attractions in a bid to get eligible young men like yourself to play the white knight and rescue her. She feels nothing for you personally. You're merely the means to an end. Fire is ill, and will use anyone in any way to attempt to leave the island.'

I recalled the occasion of our first meeting, when Fire had suggested that we elope to Earth. 'As a matter of fact she had asked me to take her away. But I refused—'

Trevellion's eyes widened fractionally. 'You did? Then I wonder what else my daughter wants from you?'

'My company?' I suggested, not wanting to believe what the fish-woman was telling me. Was my sole attraction for Fire the fact that I had access to frost?

Trevellion gave a strangled splutter deep in her altered larynx. It might have been a chortle of contempt. 'Don't flatter yourself, Benedict. Fire is using you, as you will no doubt find out. I warn you for your own good.' She inclined her head in a mock-courteous farewell. 'If I were you I would leave the island and keep away.'

She brushed past me with a susurrus of filigree fins and climbed the path to her dome. I watched her go, a sick feeling in the pit of my stomach.

I was about to head back to my launch when I saw Fire's computer board, wedged upright at my feet. Curiosity moved me to pick it up, wipe grains of sand from the screen and switch it on. Green characters glowed in the darkness.

I read the title: ' "Betrayal", by Tamara Trevellion.'

Beneath it, the poem began: 'I stand as one deserted / An alien upon Alien soil / Prey to terrors new to me . . .'

I read on for perhaps a page, but could make little sense of the extract. I dropped the board in the sand and returned to the sheltered cove and my launch, wondering if Fire's learning her mother's poetry was just one more form of psychological tyranny imposed on her by the fish-woman.

I made a conscious decision to do without frost that night. I was too concerned with thoughts of Fire to lose myself in the past. Without the drug I was prone to nightmares of the accident, but the only dreams I had that night concerned Fire Trevellion: I saw her in the arms of the next man, who could offer her both escape and the knowledge of what had happened to her sister.

I awoke late the following day, made myself a meal and sat on the patio. As the day progressed, I thought about what Tamara Trevellion had told me – and this had the effect of weakening my resolve to go without frost. It was a day since I had last taken any, and already I could feel the first symptoms of withdrawal. I was sweating slightly, and my limbs had the shakes. I felt as though I was coming down with influenza. A couple of hours later I felt even worse, and the prospect of the release that frost would bring was almost irresistible. All I had to do, I thought, was enter the lounge, ignite a little frost on the burner and find myself *elsewhere*, untroubled by thoughts of betrayal. I wanted more than anything to take the easy way out – but that, I rationalized, would be as good as admitting that I believed what Trevellion had told me about Fire's using me . . . I made myself leave the patio, take the path down to the cove and go for a long walk around the island.

As I went, I thought about my meeting with Fire that afternoon. Despite Trevellion's warnings, I would see her again today; I was too involved with her, and with her predicament on the island, to be frightened off by her mother. I recalled that I'd promised to contact Doug about the accident which had killed her sister. I returned to the lounge and got through to his office. The vid-screen flared, and Doug pulled himself towards it on a swivel-chair. He peered at me. 'Bob, you're looking terrible.'

'I'm fine,' I said. 'Had a late night, that's all. Look, I was wondering if you could help me?'

'Go on.'

'Well, you recall telling me about Jade Trevellion yesterday? I don't suppose you have the details of the accident on record?'

'I'll have them somewhere,' he said guardedly. 'Why the sudden interest?'

I shrugged. 'I saw Trevellion's daughter yesterday. We got talking about her sister's accident. She's blocked the incident from her mind, but she'd like to know what happened. I said that I'd do my best to find out, and then decide if she really should be told.'

Doug stared out of the screen at me. 'Bob, how close are you to Trevellion's daughter?'

I shrugged. 'We're just friends,' I said.

'Do you see her often?'

'Why do you ask?'

'I wonder if you could possibly make it up to Main tomorrow? I'd like to see you.'

'Sure. What about?'

'It has to do with your discovery on Brightside the other day.'

'What has that to do with Fire?'

He shook his head. 'I'll fill you in then, Bob. I think you might be able to help me.'

I shrugged. 'OK ... What time?'

'About five, say? Hold on, I'll try to get that data on the Jade case.' He pushed himself away from the screen and careered across the office to a terminal.

I was still wondering how I might be able to further help him, and how Fire might be involved, when he returned a minute later. 'Where do you want me to begin, Bob?'

'Well ... what happened, exactly?'

He frowned. 'Do you want the official version, the report my then commanding officer made public – or what he suspected really happened?'

'How about both?' I said, wondering what I was letting myself in for.

'Very well.' He glanced down at a computer board on his lap. 'The official, sanitized version is that Trevellion's daughter, Jade, slipped and fell into a sculpture she and her mother were working on. She died instantly.'

'A sculpture? Do you have any idea where the piece was situated?'

'You mean where on the island? Just a minute.' He referred to his computer. 'It was on a clearing on the southern side of the island. Why do you ask?'

I shrugged. 'Just curious, that's all ... You say she fell into it? What the hell was it made of?'

'It was a laser sculpture, Bob. It cut the girl to pieces.'

'Jesus . . .'

'Well, that's the official story. You want the Inspector's off-the-record version?'

'I'm not sure I'm looking forward to this.'

'According to the Inspector, Jade Trevellion just walked into the lasers. She committed suicide. The only witness was her sister, Fire. The Inspector questioned her and got the true version of events, but he was prevailed upon by Trevellion to release the "accident" story.'

'No wonder Fire blocked it from her memory.'

Doug was shaking his head. 'The tragedy was that Jade Trevellion had no reason to kill herself. According to the report, she was ill – she had a brain disorder which apparently was responding well to treatment – and I know for a fact that Trevellion was, and is, a rather strict parent . . . but these in themselves were no reasons for her to do what she did.' He trailed off. 'I'm glad I wasn't investigating the case, Bob. I'm flashing a pix of Jade now.'

He typed in the command, and in the top right corner of my screen appeared a colour picture of Jade Trevellion. She was sufficiently similar to Fire to take my breath away; a fresh-faced, pretty blonde-haired girl, smiling as if she hadn't a care in the world.

'Lovely kid,' Doug commented. 'What the hell possessed her?'

I cleared the pix. It was too disturbing to contemplate.

'That's about it,' he was saying. 'If I were you, I think I wouldn't give Fire Trevellion the true version of events.'

'God, I don't know.' I shrugged. 'Anyway, thanks for your help, Doug.'

'See you tomorrow at five, then.' He cut the link.

I sat and thought about Fire Trevellion and her sister. After what I'd just found out, I had no intention of allowing Fire to take frost. She had obviously blocked the incident from her mind for a reason, and who knew what harm it might do to release it with the aid of the drug? Perhaps it would be enough for her merely to *know* what had happened; perhaps the memories might return of their own accord if I told her the truth?

Around three that afternoon I steered the launch from the bay and towards Trevellion's island, wondering if a verbal account of her sister's death would satisfy Fire, or if she would insist on having the frost. Despite myself I could not help but speculate how she might react when I denied her the drug.

Physically, I was feeling much better now; the shakes had subsided and the sweating had stopped. I was relieved that I had resisted the temptation earlier to lose myself in the past.

I steered into the sheltered cove, moored the launch on the disused jetty and made my way over the headland to the beach where we had arranged to meet. The day, as ever on Meridian, was perfect. On any other occasion I might have been more appreciative of the sunlight and the clear blue skies, but this afternoon I was more than a little apprehensive at the prospect of what might pass between Fire and myself.

I had no reason to be, as things turned out. It became clear, as the beach came into sight, that I would not be meeting with Fire. At the far end of the crescent stretch of sand, diminished in the perspective, was a short, squat hovercraft. Between it and the headland on which I stood were two people: one was the tall, dominating figure of Wolfe Steiner; the other was Fire, tiny by comparison. They stood facing each other, their disproportionate figures dark against the low sun. They had the look of lovers, wrapped in a silence where no words were needed. I felt suddenly sick.

I considered approaching them – I had, after all, arranged to meet Fire here – but their intimacy stopped me. I wanted to join them so that my suspicions might be banished, but at the same time I was afraid that by doing so my worst fears might be confirmed.

They were exchanging words, lost in the distance between us. Something about their postures and attitudes suggested an end-of-affair confrontation: Steiner was imposing, almost threatening; from time to time he made gestures which might have accompanied pleas. Fire stood with her head bowed, occasionally lifting it to give quick glances. There was a certain air of sullenness on her part, indicating someone reluctant to be cajoled by a lover's entreaties. Or was I, in my jealousy, reading more into the tête-à-tête than was actually there?

Fire looked up then and defiantly shook her head. Steiner reached out and took her by the shoulders. She seemed to stiffen. He drew her head to his chest, stroking her hair.

At this, Fire pulled away, broke free of his embrace. She cried something at him, which cheered me with its vehemence, although all I heard was: 'No . . .'

In a show of emotion quite alien to him, Steiner almost shouted: 'Don't you realize . . .' but the rest of the sentence failed to reach me.

Fire shook her head, avoiding his eyes.

At this, he grabbed Fire's shoulders and rattled her. Fire went lax, and as if in horror at what he had done, Steiner released her. She slipped gracefully to the sand.

I was about to run from the headland and confront the Director when I saw three figures emerge from the shadows at the foot of the cliff and approach Steiner and the prostrate girl. I recognized the obese surgeon; he was accompanied by two uniformed security guards.

The surgeon knelt with difficulty and examined Fire, alternating his probes with questions directed at Steiner. The guards had drawn their weapons; Steiner looked distinctly uneasy. At a word from the surgeon, the guards replaced their pistols. Between them they picked up Fire and carried her carefully up the beach towards the steps that led to Trevellion's dome.

The surgeon remained with Steiner; there was a brief, heated exchange, before the surgeon turned and hurried up the beach. He caught up with the guards and fussed with the unconscious girl as they climbed the steps. Director Steiner watched them go, then strode along the beach to the hovercraft. The vehicle rose, turned and sped away from the island.

I returned to my launch. I could not clear from my mind Steiner's obvious affection for Fire, which suggested a certain intimacy in the past. As I made my way home, I told myself that I should not feel betrayed – there was in all likelihood a reasonable explanation for everything I had observed. But some other, suspicious part of me could not forget what Tamara Trevellion had told me the evening before.

The half-shell of frost awaited me on the coffee table, beckoning. To coincide with my arrival home, stomach cramps and nausea had taken hold of me. It was all I could do to hurry through the lounge and lock myself in the bedroom. I spent a fitful night and awoke in the morning feeling like a victim of the plague.

4

MAIN ISLAND

Two hundred kilometres and almost as many islands separated my home base from Main, the largest land mass of the archipelago. The garden city, if the settlement could be called a city, occupied all the island, a collection of one-storey quake-safe buildings and wide tree-lined streets. The Telemass station was situated on a small neighbouring isle connected to Main by a suspension bridge.

I set off an hour or so after dawn that morning and arrived just before noon. I had a few hours to kill before my meeting with Doug Foulds, so I decided to take a trip out to the Telemass station. I had left home early in the hope that a change of environment might bring about a corresponding change of mind: whenever I thought of Fire, which was more often than not, I experienced a sensation equivalent to emotional nausea. I was beginning to wish that I'd never set eyes on the girl. My life before our meeting had been, if solitary, at least straightforward and uncomplicated.

I drove across the suspension bridge, left the launch in the parking lot and bought a visitor's pass from the kiosk beneath the three towering scimitar legs of the station. A glass elevator pod rushed me and a dozen other sightseers up the tripod. From this altitude, the archipelago curved away on either side, a diminishing series of emeralds embedded in a strip of brilliant lapis lazuli.

The elevator halted and I stepped out on to a gallery overlooking the hexagonal operations area, marked with arcane hieroglyphs and busy with blue-uniformed technicians. This was only the second time I had visited the station since my arrival on Meridian, and once again its working end reminded me of nothing so much as the deck and superstructure of a battleship. I leaned against the padded rail that ran the length of the glassed-in gallery, surrounded by tourists, retirees, and schoolchildren, and watched grab-trucks ferry crates from the goods elevator to the centre of the pad. A large countdown monitor, set high on the opposite control tower, ticked off the minutes and seconds to the time of the next shot. The light show was just thirty minutes away.

As colony planets went, Meridian was insignificant. We produced nothing that Earth could not do without, and imported from Earth all the foodstuffs we required to survive. I could appreciate the logic behind Earth's decision to scale down the Telemass operations to and from Meridian. Each trans-stellar shot cost billions of credits and, as Earth sustained a massive network of Telemass links throughout the Expansion, it was understandable that it should wish to limit expenditure on some of the smaller worlds. As I watched the final preparations for the outward shot, I thought about how the scale-down might affect the planet. The reduction of shots from three to one a month meant, in real terms, a corresponding reduction of supplies by a third. All non-essential imports would have to be dropped, and a priority given to food supplies. The majority of materials used by the artists on Meridian were imported from Earth, and I wondered how a reduction might affect them. I foresaw a sudden exodus of artists from Meridian – and without its artists, the planet's economy would collapse. I hoped that my vision was ill-founded, a result of my mood that morning.

My thoughts were interrupted by the countdown from the public address system. The centre of the deck below us was stacked with a tall ziggurat of containers; as we watched, these containers began to glow. They lost their geometric definition and became shapeless, then dissolved into a million points of fizzing golden light, which brightened and rose to form a tall, spectacular column. Then the dazzling bolt streaked away into the heavens at the start of its fraction-of-a-second journey to Earth. Perhaps the most incredible thing about the shot was that it was accomplished in absolute silence. The spectators in the gallery drew breaths of delight and applauded.

Technicians swarmed across the pad again, lifted covers in the deck and began work on the revealed machinery. A voice over the tannoy announced the arrival of a shot from Earth in a little over one hour.

I moved along to the bar, bought a drink, and positioned myself by the viewscreen. The palsy that I'd awoken with that morning was wearing off, and I was beginning to feel a little better. I wondered how long it would be before the next bout of sickness, and if the withdrawal symptoms would get worse before they ceased altogether. I had never before gone for so long without frost.

As I sat, I found myself glancing up with interest every time a station official came into view below. Only when I saw Wolfe Steiner stride across the deck and climb the steps to the bar did I begin to wonder if the reason I had come here today was to seek out the Director. At the sight of him, I suddenly had to know what his meeting with Fire had been about. I might have been reluctant to approach the imposing figure of the Director before yesterday, but his display on the beach of attributes I had not ascribed to him, like tenderness and concern, made him somehow approachable.

He was in conversation with Weller, the bearded technical adviser – sporting dark glasses today – I had seen at the event the other evening. Steiner stood stiffly at the bar, a non-alcoholic drink in his hand. As always when observed over a period, he gave the impression that from time to time he was entirely elsewhere, listening rapt to the siren song of his implant.

I waited until the adviser finished his drink and left, then I crossed to the bar and stood beside Steiner under the pretext of ordering another drink. The Director seemed oblivious of my presence; his eyes were distant as points of light sequenced across his carotid spar. When he emerged from his reverie and took a drink, I caught his gaze and nodded.

His enquiry was brusque, almost brutal, and altogether in keeping with his mechanical demeanour. 'Have we met?'

I smiled in sardonic acknowledgement of his civility. 'At Tamara Trevellion's party a few nights ago—'

He regarded me sternly, as if attempting to judge the threat I represented. 'What do you want, Mr . . . ?'

'Benedict. Bob Benedict. I'm a friend of Fire Trevellion.'

He took a sip of his drink, wholly non-committal. 'And how might I help you, Mr Benedict?'

I decided to go for the diplomatic approach. 'Well, I was hoping that you might be able to tell me something about her, Director.'

Steiner smiled without humour. 'You were?'

'You must know her rather well. Weren't you once a good friend of Tamara Trevellion?'

'I fail to see how that qualifies me in your eyes as someone who knows anything about her daughter.'

'But you do know her?'

His expression flashed impatience. 'What exactly do you want, Mr Benedict?'

'I saw you on the beach yesterday,' I began.

His response was swift. 'Did Tamara Trevellion put you up to this?'

'I assure you, I dislike Trevellion as much as you do. All I'm bothered about is Fire.'

'Is that so?' His expression was patronizing now, almost amused. 'Then I hope you have more luck than I did.'

I was bemused. I recalled the evident concern with which he had treated Fire yesterday. 'Were you close to her?' I asked.

Steiner laughed uncharacteristically. 'Not at all – I pity her. I was trying to get her to leave the island, if you must know. Are you in the habit of spying on Fire and everyone she meets?'

'I was due to meet her there myself,' I explained. I went on, 'Anyway, she won't leave the island because of her illness. Hasn't she told you about that? She's being treated by her mother's surgeon, at great expense.'

'That's what she told you, is it?' he said, watching me closely. 'Then again, why not? That's probably what she believes.'

My stomach turned. 'What do you mean?'

'I mean simply that Fire Trevellion is not in command of her reality. She is controlled wholly by her mother. She might tell you what she genuinely believes to be the truth, but the subjective determinants of that truth are governed by Tamara. Don't forget that she has been on the island, under her mother's unwavering influence, for every day of her life.'

I shook my head. 'You make her sound like a puppet,' I said.

Steiner lifted his lips in a parody of a smile. 'That's a very good description, Mr Benedict. Fire is a puppet of Tamara Trevellion's warped sensibilities, caught up in a scenario she has no way of understanding.' He hesitated. 'A word of advice. If I were you, I'd stay well clear of Trevellion and her daughter. Tamara is a cruel and dangerous woman, and Fire is so unwitting and naïve that she is almost as dangerous herself.' He regarded the countdown display through the viewscreen. 'Mr Benedict, I really must be going. I hope you take note of what I've said.'

I remained at the bar for a long time, staring into my drink. In effect, Steiner had told me nothing that I had not already worked out for myself, even if his presentation of the facts was a little more forceful. I had been aware of Fire's subordination to her mother, but it had taken the view of a third party to bring home the extent of Trevellion's control. Even so, I considered Steiner's warning, if well meant, vague enough to ignore. I suspected that he was thinking back to his own disastrous involvement with Tamara Trevellion when he counselled me to leave well alone.

As I left the Telemass station and drove across the suspension bridge to Main Island it came to me that, beneath his augmentation and rather severe formality, Director Steiner was human after all.

I still had some time to kill before my meeting with Doug, so I settled the launch outside a boulevard café and sat at a table in the sunlight. I ordered a light meal – one effect of the withdrawals was to reduce my appetite – and watched the citizens of Main promenading down the wide tree-lined avenue. The majority were normals, with the occasional Altered and Augmented for variety. After the seclusion of my own island, where often I might go for weeks without seeing a soul, it was a strange sensation to be among so many people and yet still alone. I told myself that immediately upon my return I really should look up Abe or Fire . . .

My involvement with Fire served only to emphasize the fact that my isolation, which for so long had been my natural and preferred state, was coming to an end. I was entering uncharted territory, and while part of me welcomed the change, another could not help but feel afraid.

Along the boulevard, outside an electrical goods supplier, a long low-loader settled to the ground with a sigh of deflated skirts. A dozen men and women in white overalls, their backs bearing the logo of the retailer, began floating large crates on to the bed of the juggernaut. One piece of machinery was not crated: a satellite dish or small radio telescope.

I had been watching the loading operation for a minute or two before I realized that the tall dark figure supervising the procedure was familiar. She was monitoring the loading with the hauteur of one to whom such physical work was anathema. She might have been any Altered fish-woman, but something in her overbearing attitude told me that it could only be Tamara Trevellion. I considered the irony of travelling two hundred kilometres only to happen across my least favourite person on the planet. I wondered what new project she was embarking upon which required so much technical apparatus.

I drained my beer and was about to settle my bill and leave when I was jumped from behind. Someone pressed warm fingers over my eyes. 'You don't get away that easy, Mr Benedict! Guess who?'

I touched her hand. 'Fire?' I was aware that my hand was shaking, and pulled it quickly away.

'Right first time.' She fell into a seat across the table and gestured around her. 'Isn't it a great day? I love the city!' She was wearing a bright yellow trouser-suit, with a tight bodice and flaring pants. The outfit was years behind the times and gave her the appearance of an invalid out on day release – which, in a way, she was. 'What a coincidence meeting you here!'

I smiled. I was struck at how animated Fire was away from her mother. Watching her, I felt again that dangerous surge of jealousy which I had first experienced last night on seeing Fire and Steiner together on the beach.

'I don't often get up here,' she went on, looking over her shoulder to where her mother was chastising a worker over some supposed misdemeanour. She frowned, then smiled dazzlingly at me. 'But when I do I make the most of it. Look – Tamara hasn't given me any creds today, and I'm starving. Do you think you could buy me a meal? I'll pay you back later. I have some savings . . .'

I passed her the menu and enjoyed watching her regard the list with confusion. She looked up, shook her head – 'There's so much . . .' – then returned to the menu with renewed concentration.

When she had finally made her selection – a sea-food salad – she sat back with satisfaction and smiled at me. 'Last time I was here I wandered off and got lost. Tamara was frantic. When she found me she said she'd never bring me here again.'

'Why did she relent?'

Fire smiled. 'Maybe she doesn't trust me alone on the island with you around.'

Her manner evoked memories of three days ago, when she had suggested with flippant bravado that we elope. The only way she knew of hinting at a better life was to make it the subject of a joke.

I indicated the juggernaut. 'What's Tamara buying?' I asked. 'A radar to keep me away?'

Fire shrugged, as if the last thing she wanted to discuss was her mother. 'I don't know . . . It's some special broadcaster, I think. She plans to beam her events to Earth in future, instead of sending tapes. I'm sure the citizens of Earth will be just *delighted*.'

Her meal arrived, and its abundance fazed her as had the menu. For a while she busied herself eating, watching me between mouthfuls.

'Hey' – she bobbed her head, wide-eyed, in conjunction with a gulp – 'are you OK, Mr Benedict?'

She was obviously referring to the sweat which had broken out on my face. I felt queasy. 'I'm fine,' I said.

She peered. 'You don't look too well.'

'I'll survive.'

She smiled. 'So . . . what brings you to Main?'

I had been wondering for some time how to broach the subject of her meeting with Steiner. I said, 'Well, I was so disappointed after yesterday that I decided to come here and drown my sorrows.' I lifted my glass.

She frowned until half-way through the sentence and then, as understanding hit her, she regarded the half-eaten mess of her salad with downcast eyes.

'I arrived early,' I said. 'I saw you on the beach with the Director.'

Her eyes were wide, frightened. She tried to regain her composure with a negligent shrug. 'But you should have come along anyway. It might have stopped what happened later – I had a fainting fit. It happens sometimes.'

'What did Steiner want?'

She regarded her plate again. 'He asked me to leave with him,' she murmured.

'Leave the island?' I asked. 'Join him here on Main?' My tone was incredulous. Steiner had said nothing earlier about Fire's leaving *with* him.

Fire was shaking her head, still not looking me in the eye. She said in a voice so soft I had to lean forward to hear her words: 'He wanted me to leave the planet with him next week, go with him to his next posting.'

I stared at her; a rivulet of sweat ran down my neck and over my chest. I recalled Steiner telling me that all he felt for Fire was pity. I felt a surge of jealousy, and hated myself for it.

'But didn't he want Tamara to leave with him the other week?' I asked. 'She refused . . . so he asked you?'

She shrugged. 'Look' – she hesitated – 'it goes back further than that. Five, six years ago he had a thing going with Jade. They saw a lot of each other, though Tamara did her best to put a stop to it. Then Jade . . . then she had the accident.' She paused, then went on, 'A year ago, after my father went missing, Steiner returned to the island. It was as if he felt personally responsible for what had happened to my father. Tamara hated him at first, but then . . . well, gradually she came to like him, maybe even to love him – at least that's what I thought then. After the event the other night, I know my mother was playing him along all the time.'

I considered Steiner's strange obsession with the Trevellion women. I could understand any man's interest in Fire and Jade, but how anyone could be attracted to Tamara Trevellion was beyond me. 'What do you think Steiner felt for your mother?' I asked.

Fire pushed out her lips, considering. 'Oh' – she sounded tired – 'at the time I thought he genuinely loved her. Maybe I was just hoping he might take the place of the father I'd lost. He took all the abuse that Tamara could throw at him, even though he remained, you know, *distant*. He seemed interested in her not as a person, but as an artist. He wanted to know all about her art. Then . . .' She lapsed into silence.

'Then?'

She shrugged. 'He began to take an interest in me. Whenever he called in at the island he always insisted on seeing me for an hour or two. A couple of times he offered to take me shopping to Main, but Tamara wouldn't allow that.'

'Perhaps he felt responsible for you, after the accident? Was he aware of how badly Tamara treated you?'

'He wasn't blind. He saw all that. It was as if he was trying to compensate for her spitefulness by being kind.' She looked up. 'He never touched me, nothing like that. But I still didn't like all his attention.'

'I should have thought that after so long without affection . . .'

She shrugged, frowned. 'I don't know. It was strange, weird, all his concern after so long without it from anyone. It was as if he *pitied* me for who I was – and I resented that. I didn't want his pity. Then, a few months ago, he suggested that I should go with him when he left Meridian. He painted a fine picture of all the wonders of the Expansion I'd be able to experience, insisted that I join him.'

'But you refused?'

She trawled her fork aimlessly through the food on her plate. 'I told him I couldn't possibly go – I needed treatment for my condition. He said that surgeons on Earth would be able to cure me completely, no more tests and monitoring. I'd be free.'

'So . . . what stopped you?' I pressed.

'Tamara found out. She wouldn't let me see him, after that. And anyway, I don't think I would have gone. I don't really like him. He's too' – she searched for the word – 'too *distant*, mechanical.'

Then she looked up at me, popped a prawn into her mouth and chewed. She changed the subject. 'Oh, have you found out what happened to Jade yet, like you said you would?'

My stomach felt as though it had suddenly turned to lead.

She saw my expression. 'What is it?' Her voice faltered.

I wanted more than anything to tell her that I had forgotten to ask Doug Foulds, but the look of entreaty in her eyes would not allow the lie. I had to tell her the truth – but, of course, there were two versions of the truth. I had the urge to tell Fire the 'official' version of her sister's death, which ascribed the tragedy to an accident. But the danger of telling her the least harrowing scenario might be that Fire would demand the drug so that she could relive her part in the experience.

I had to tell her the truth.

'Well, Mr Benedict? What did the Inspector say?'

'I spoke to Doug Foulds yesterday,' I said. 'He didn't investigate the case – his superior did.'

'So he doesn't know what happened?'

I hesitated. 'He looked up the records and gave me the outline of his superior's report.'

'And?'

I avoided her eyes. 'This might be hard for you to take—'

'I want to know the truth, Mr Benedict.'

'Very well.' I paused, wondering how to phrase it. 'Tamara was working with Jade on a laser sculpture in the glade you took me to the other evening. When the accident happened, your mother called in the then Inspector to investigate. He found out what happened – but Tamara didn't want the true version of the tragedy to be known. He released a report which stated that Jade fell into the sculpture and died instantly . . .'

She stared at me. 'And the truth?'

'The truth, according to the report, was that Jade walked in the sculpture voluntarily. She took her own life.'

Fire looked stricken. She was slowly shaking her head.

'No . . . no. She wouldn't have done such a thing. Why would she do *that*?'

'I'm sorry, Fire.'

She gripped my hand imploringly. 'Is it possible that the Inspector got it wrong – that it *was* an accident, after all?'

'Fire . . .' I didn't know where to begin. My mouth was suddenly dry. I took a long drink of beer and looked anywhere except into her green, beseeching eyes.

'Fire, you were the only witness to what happened. You were there when Jade – when she did what she did. The Inspector questioned you, and you told him what you had seen.'

Fire just stared at her plate, open-mouthed with shock.

'It's obvious why you blocked it from your mind, why you can't recall what happened. Can't you see that?'

'I just can't believe that Jade took her own life,' she murmured.

'Perhaps if I get you a copy of the official report. We could return to the clearing one evening and go through your statement. Perhaps that might bring something back—'

'There is an easier way,' she began.

'Fire . . .'

'Let me have the frost, Mr Benedict. I want to relive the experience. I couldn't take it back then because I was young and close to Jade. I'm older now. I know what happened to her – but I want to *see* it.'

'I couldn't allow that. It might be far too dangerous. You blocked it originally for a reason. To experience it now might be more than you could take. Imagine the terror of reliving her death a second time.'

'I survived it once, Mr Benedict. I want the memory of what happened!'

'It's more than just the memory. You'd relive the actual event. You'd be fifteen again, loving Jade, and when she . . . when she died, you'd feel all the horror that you experienced the first time. God knows what it'd do to you.'

'You just can't imagine the hell of not knowing.'

'But you *know* what happened.' I was exasperated. 'What more do you want?'

She stared at her fingers. 'I just want to satisfy myself, that's all.'

'Fire, I'll get a transcription of your statement. If we go through it, over and over, perhaps something might return. It'd be safer than taking frost. Please believe me, I'm on your side. I just don't want to see you hurt.' I attempted to take her hands across the table, but she drew them away.

She looked up. 'So you won't give me the drug, Mr Benedict?'

I shook my head. 'I can't.'

She was silent for a long time, staring blindly at the table-top. I could not help but recall what Tamara Trevellion had said the other night, that Fire was using me, with the implication that she would drop me if she got what she wanted, or did not . . .

Then Fire did a surprising thing. She reached across the table, took my hand and squeezed. 'Hey, Mr Benedict – don't look so down, OK?' She shrugged. 'I understand why you won't let me have the stuff. Maybe you're right. Perhaps I should try to recall what happened some other way.' And she smiled so genuinely that I was ashamed of the suspicion Tamara Trevellion had planted in my head.

I recalled what Fire had told me, that the work of art Tamara and Jade had been working on was now exhibited at a museum on Main.

'If you like,' I said, 'perhaps we could visit the museum here sometime, see the piece your mother and Jade created? You never know, it might help.'

'That'd be great.' Her tone was enthusiastic, but I could see the doubt in her eyes.

Behind her, the last of the crates was being manoeuvred into position on the back of the low-loader. Tamara Trevellion was going through various documents with the store manager. She initialled the final receipt, then began looking around, presumably for Fire.

I asked quickly, 'What are you doing over the next couple of days?'

She shrugged. 'Not much. Why?'

'How would you like to go gliding with me?'

'I'd love to.' From delight at the prospect, her expression turned glum. 'But Tamara wouldn't let me.'

'Do you have to tell her? Couldn't you just sneak off for a few hours?'

Fire sighed. 'And face her anger when I got back?'

'Aren't you accustomed to it by now? Wouldn't it be worth it? Have you ever been gliding before?'

She shook her head, tracing a pattern on the table-top. 'I've never even flown before. Do you own a glider?'

'A two-berth model. I bought it when I first arrived – I went out every week in the early days. We could set off early one day, come here and visit the museum.'

Fire remained staring at the water pattern she had made with her finger. 'It's impossible, Mr Benedict. You don't understand what Tamara might do when I got back.'

'Withhold your treatment?' I laughed. 'Fire, perhaps the reason she's so cruel is that you put up with it. Perhaps if you stood your ground, fought back—'

'You don't understand—' a whisper. 'Do you know what she did to me last month, when I accidentally dropped one of her crystals? She gave me the nightmares.'

I almost laughed. 'The . . . *what?*'

'I don't know how she does it. Maybe she puts something in my food or drink. Then when I go to sleep, I dream that I'm in the sea near Darkside and it's night-time and a fish like a shark is attacking me, tearing me to pieces. It's always the same dream, and it always comes after I've done something wrong.'

'Your mother,' I said, 'is a monster.'

'I hate her so much that I pity her, Mr Benedict.'

I stared at the disconsolate girl for a while before saying, 'The only thing that keeps you with your mother is your illness, right?'

She gave a grudging nod.

'What would you say if I arranged an appointment with a specialist here on Main?'

She shrugged. 'What good would that do?'

'Well, you might find out exactly what's wrong with you. You have only Tamara's word for it that your treatment is expensive. For all you know, it might be relatively cheap. If that were so . . .'

'I don't know,' she began.

'What have you got to lose? If you could be treated by an independent doctor, at moderate cost . . . That would mean you'd be free. You could live anywhere you liked.'

'Anywhere? Anywhere at all?'

'Anywhere. What do you say?'

'I'm frightened. I've never defied Tamara before.'

'Do you want to spend the rest of your life imprisoned on the island with your mother?'

Tamara Trevellion had spotted us and was approaching along the tree-lined boulevard.

'Here she comes,' I said. 'Brace yourself.'

Trevellion paused before our table. I knew it was only in my mind, but her sudden presence seemed to reduce the temperature by twenty degrees. I was repulsed by the sight of the sucker-fish swarming over her body.

Beside me Fire shivered, shrank into herself.

'So here you are, Fire,' Trevellion snapped. 'Benedict – you obviously go to inordinate lengths to arrange a rendezvous.'

'We met by accident,' I said. 'I had no idea you were here.'

Trevellion lowered herself into a seat at the table, arranging her frills and fronds as she would the fine silk of an expensive gown. She transferred her attention to me. 'As it happens, Benedict, you are the very man I need to see.'

I stared at her, suspicious. 'I am?'

'For a long time now I have been wanting to add to my menagerie of native Meridian fauna. At the event the other day I asked Abraham Cunningham if he might procure me a sand lion. For reasons of his own, he declined to do so. None the less, I still desire a specimen. I was wondering . . .' she gave me what I took to be a calculating look, 'would you be prepared to capture me one and deliver it to my island?'

Fire burst in, 'No, you can't, Bob. It's too dangerous!'

Trevellion turned a cold gaze on her daughter. 'Be silent! This is Mr Benedict's decision.'

I wondered why Trevellion had singled me out as the one person, after Abe, suited to capturing a lion. I considered everything Abe had told me about the animals. In any other situation I might have told the woman what to do with her request.

'Fire's right,' I said. 'It's a very dangerous job.'

'And one for which you would be amply rewarded,' Trevellion said.

'I don't want payment,' I said. 'That is, monetary payment.'

'Bob!' Fire almost wailed.

Trevellion ignored her daughter, regarded me with cold, inhuman eyes. 'Oh, and in what manner might you require payment, Benedict?'

'I'd like to take Fire gliding,' I said.

Fire regarded me, wide-eyed.

Trevellion asked, 'I take it you are a qualified pilot?'

'I can fly everything from gliders to bigships.'

Trevellion turned to her daughter. 'Do you wish to go gliding with Mr Benedict?' she asked.

Fire opened her mouth, but no words came. She nodded mutely.

'In that case, I can really see no objection to your accompanying Benedict on a flight.'

'When do you want the lion?' I asked.

'As soon as possible, Benedict. Say . . . tomorrow?'

'And when can Fire come gliding?'

'How would the day after suit you? If, that is, you deliver the lion.'

I nodded. 'That seems reasonable enough.'

Trevellion graciously inclined her head. 'That's settled, then. I look forward to seeing you tomorrow. Fire, it's time we were leaving.

Benedict . . .' She rose and strode away from the table, sunlight scintillating across her scales.

Fire followed obediently, but not before looking back at me with an expression that was equal parts pleasure and pain. They climbed into a chauffeur-driven limousine. The vehicle rose and moved off down the boulevard, followed by the juggernaut.

As I watched them go, I contemplated the prospect of capturing a sand lion – all for the chance of spending time alone with Fire Trevellion.

The Meridian Law Enforcement Agency had its headquarters in a modest two-storey office block on the coast road, overlooking a secluded bay on the sunward side of the island. I settled my launch in the parking lot and strolled into the carpeted foyer. A receptionist showed me to Doug's office on the second floor.

'Bob, good to see you.' He ushered me into a plush hospitality lounge adjacent to his office. In the confines of the room, his bulk emphasized by the absence of space, he seemed even smaller and broader than ever.

'I'm sorry to drag you all the way up here.'

'That's OK. I was doing nothing better. I made a day of it.'

He poured a couple of beers and we stood before the floor-to-ceiling viewscreen, admiring the panorama. To our right, the archipelago curved away into the distance. Before us, the wastes of Brightside burned with a fierce actinic glare. I thought of the journey I would be making tomorrow.

'How's the investigation coming along?' I asked.

'It's progressing slowly,' he said. 'Very slowly.' He seemed more sombre than his usual jovial self.

'So you still think Abe and I were hallucinating?' I laughed.

Doug smiled. 'As a matter of fact I don't,' he said. 'One or two things have come to light which tend to corroborate your claims.'

'Such as?' I sipped my beer.

'We ran a few forensic tests on the scrap of uniform you found. Through tissue samples and sweat specimens, we traced who it belonged to. Or, rather, we *know* who it belonged to. We're ninety-nine per cent certain that it's the property of Deputy Director Hannah Rodriguez, second in command at the Telemass station.'

'Have you found her?'

'That's the thing. According to Director Steiner, Rodriguez began a month's leave a week ago. She was a keen sailor – she mentioned to Steiner and her co-workers at the station that she was planning a trip down south past the equator. Apparently, she set off five days ago. We've checked the marina where she kept her catamaran, but there's no sign of the boat. I've had a spotter-plane checking the sea from here to the equator, but they haven't found the craft. She seems to have disappeared without a trace.'

'So the body we saw could have been hers?'

Doug nodded. 'Someone took her out there, killed her and left the body to the lions. They could have scuttled the boat, to make it look like she's been lost at sea. Perhaps they returned to Brightside later, once it became known that you'd found something, and somehow got rid of all the evidence.'

I finished my beer. 'Is this what you wanted to see me about?'

He crossed the room to a desk, picked up a silver envelope and passed it to me. I withdrew the pix of an olive-skinned, dark-haired woman in her early forties. She was pictured on the deck of the Telemass station, wearing the light-blue uniform of the organization.

'Hannah Rodriguez?'

'Taken a couple of years ago, just after her arrival on Meridian.'

'How can I help?' I asked.

'Rodriguez was a friend of Tamara Trevellion's. She was something of an amateur artist and she liked Trevellion's work. She was a regular guest at the island, up to the time of her disappearance. Rodriguez was something of a loner – none of her colleagues at the station claimed they really knew her. It occurred to me that Trevellion or her daughter might know something about her, something which might shed light on the mystery.'

'Surely you don't suspect Tamara Trevellion?'

'Let's put it this way – I suspect everyone who'd ever had anything to do with Rodriguez. It's safer that way. I've already been down to question Trevellion but she was giving nothing away.'

'What do you want me to do?'

'I thought perhaps you could ask Fire how the women got along, if there were ever any differences of opinion. She might even know if Rodriguez had enemies, people she didn't trust. Anything like that. I'll be interviewing her later, but she might be more open with you.'

I nodded. 'I'll do that. I'm seeing her in the next day or two.'

'Good. I really need to know more about Rodriguez. At the moment I know next to nothing, least of all why someone might want her dead.' Doug looked tired, his features drawn. 'Now, how about another beer?'

Thirty minutes later I stepped from the building and entered a vid-booth in the parking lot. I got through to the surgery of a neuro-specialist and made an appointment for Fire in two days' time. Then I returned to my launch and sat for a while, staring out at the sea and the islands and thinking through my meeting with Fire, Tamara Trevellion, and Doug. Little by little, I was being drawn into a situation of involvement which, mere days ago, I would have viewed with alarm.

The only cause for alarm I had now was that I was beginning to enjoy the position in which I found myself.

5

BRIGHTSIDE REVISITED

I awoke the following morning feeling ill, overcome with hot and cold sweats. I tried to eat breakfast, but half-way through had to rush to the bathroom and vomit. My stomach felt a little better after that, but the pain that wracked the rest of my body persisted, increasing in severity as the morning progressed.

I lay on the chesterfield and fought the cramps. The sparkling pink powder in the half-shell was a constant temptation. I wanted to give in, seek the solace of frost. Why was I torturing myself like this? My life before I encountered Fire, an existence of isolation, apathy, and relatively good health, seemed rather attractive now . . . Forget Fire, I told myself – don't risk your life attempting to snare a sand lion; stay on your island, seek refuge in frost and let the affairs of the world continue without you . . . I had gone without frost for two nights now and the nightmares of the accident had stayed away. But I wondered how long that might last, how long before I suffered an epic nightmare that brought back all the horror, pain and guilt? How easy it would be to rid myself of the physical pain, and the threat of mental anguish, by burning a line of frost and finding myself . . . *elsewhere*.

Then I realized where these thoughts were leading me, and I saw in my mind's eye Fire's expression of delight at the prospect of going gliding with me. I almost ran from the dome and down the path to the jetty. I boarded my launch, cast off, and accelerated across the open sea before I could change my mind.

Abe's battered flier was parked on the quayside when I steered into the bay fifteen minutes later. I settled my launch beside it, climbed out, and made my way up the steep pathway to the villa. I paused half-way, less to admire the view than to rest. I felt weak; the heat was draining me.

I sat on a rock beside the path, surrounded by the calls of a dozen different animals, and stared out across the ocean to the mirage-shimmering landmass of Brightside and, beyond, the curtain of fire that danced on the horizon. The knowledge that today I would have to make the journey into the inhospitable wilderness did not appeal, and not for the first time I began to wonder if what I was doing made sense.

I continued up the path to the verandah overlooking the steep incline and the sea. Abe was standing before the low wall, staring out across the sea. A pair of binoculars hung on a strap around his neck. I thought I'd caught him in a moment of private introspection, even sadness. He turned and smiled when he saw me. 'Bob, can I get you something?'

'I could do with a juice.'

'How are you?' he asked, standing by the dispenser with his back to me.

I hesitated. 'Fine,' I said. 'I'm getting out a bit more, seeing Fire Trevellion.'

He passed me the drink. He looked dubious. 'What does Tamara have to say about that? She's notorious for not giving Fire any leeway.'

'She was a bit cold at first. She's relented a little now.'

I wondered if now was the right time to mention that I needed his advice about the sand lion. I was about to tell him about Tamara Trevellion's request when I noticed his expression. He was watching me with a kind of paternal concern.

'What is it?' I asked.

'Bob, I don't want to see you get hurt.'

His words sent a chill down my spine.

I shrugged, laughed. 'Tamara can't hurt me,' I said.

Abe shook his head. 'It's not Tamara I'm thinking about. I mean Fire.'

'Fire's OK,' I said.

Abe leaned back against the rail, regarded his drink. 'Bob . . . let me tell you something. You might not like me for it.'

I stared at him. 'What is it?'

'Last year, just after Pat died, Tamara invited me over a few times, to parties and events and things. Of course I met Fire while I was there. We got on well. I was still getting over my loss, and Fire was without a father . . .'

'What happened?' I took a drink, nervous.

'We saw a lot of each other. She knew I made frequent trips Brightside and she asked me to take her. Well, I was quite willing, but Tamara vetoed the idea. A week or two later, Fire asked me to bring her some frost flowers back from Brightside the next time I went. She told me she wanted to know more about how her sister died. I refused, of course. I thought the idea was sick and I told her so. After that, she didn't want to see me again. I admit, I felt hurt. I suppose I looked on Fire as the daughter I never had.'

I smiled, relieved. 'I know all about her wanting frost. She asked me for it too. I refused to give her any – but it didn't seem to make any difference. She still wants to see me.'

Abe smiled. 'Then I'm happy for you. Fire's obviously found someone who matters to her, not just some old father figure.' He paused. 'What does Tamara think about you two . . . ?'

'At first she warned me against trespassing on her island and seeing Fire. Then yesterday she said I could take Fire gliding.'

'Quite a change of mind.'

'Well, I did agree to do something for her. That's why I'm here. I need your advice.'

'How can I help?'

'Remember the event at Trevellion's? She asked you if you'd be willing to catch her a sand lion. She still wants one. She said that if I captured her one, I could take Fire gliding.'

'And you agreed?'

'I intend to go over to Brightside today and bring one back.'

'Just like that?' Abe smiled to himself.

'Well, I need your advice, of course.'

'Did Tamara tell you why she wanted a lion?'

I shrugged. 'As a pet, I presume.'

'As a status symbol, more like. She's had everything else. A pet sand lion on a leash would cause quite a stir in her social circles.' He paused and glanced across at me. 'Bob, why didn't you just refuse Trevellion's request – continue meeting Fire clandestinely?'

I made a lame gesture. 'I don't know. Perhaps subconsciously I feared that Fire might not go on seeing me, if her mother turned the screws. She's got a strange hold over the girl. Anyway, I came here to ask you how I should go about bagging the lion.'

Abe finished his drink, strolled over to the dispenser and collected another. He seemed to be considering. He leaned against the rail that encircled the patio. 'There are two main ways of going about it,' he began. 'One relatively safe, the other less so.'

'What's the safer method?'

'Simple. You just take a cage a hundred kilometres into Brightside, load it with meat and leave it. A couple of days later you go back, and nine times out of ten you've got yourself a lion.'

'I did say I'd bring her one back today.'

'In that case you want the other method. You take a laser rifle and a specially adapted cage, go out to where the lions scavenge, and shoot one. With luck, it'll stay down long enough to let you position the cage over it and ensnare the animal. But it's risky.'

'I don't know if I like the sound of it,' I said.

'The disadvantage with this method is that ideally there should be two people with rifles. And preferably one of them should be experienced.'

'I can't let you come with me, Abe. I got myself into this.'

'I couldn't let you go out there alone, for chrissake. Anyway, there's something happening on Brightside I want to take a look at while we're there.'

'Oh?' Instinctively, I looked across the ocean to the line of the horizon. All I could make out was the constant, dancing wall of fire.

'If you look slightly to the left of centre, just below the aurora.'

I stared, and five seconds later was rewarded by the sight of a quick, lateral spear of light, for all the world like laser fire, describe a line parallel to the horizon.

'Here, you can see it better through these.' He passed me the binoculars, and after a short wait I made out another linear streak of light, bending around the distant curve of the hemisphere. The sight was maddeningly familiar.

'It's been going on for the last hour,' Abe told me. 'They're Telemass bolts, coming in from the south and terminating in the vicinity of the old Solar Research building.'

'Any idea what's happening?'

He shook his head. 'Search me. We'll take my truck, snare a lion and then take a look on the way back, OK?'

We changed into silversuits, armed ourselves with laser rifles, and loaded the cage on to the back of the hover-truck. Abe accelerated the vehicle from the bay and for the next hour we made good progress across the calm sea. Ahead, the flat, ochreous foreshore of Brightside shimmered and vibrated like the strummed string of a musical instrument. On the far horizon the line of dancing fire, presided over by the blazing disc of Beta Hydri, burned purple patches on our retinas.

Beside me, Abe gripped the wheel and gave a nervous commentary; this volubility was quite unlike him, and I could only assume that he was fazed at the thought of capturing a sand lion.

'There's been a lot of sunspot activity over the past couple of days,' he said, 'hence the aurora. The temperature is always ten to twenty degrees above the average when this happens.'

He went on to tell me that the truck wasn't insulated – as the flier had been the other day – or the windscreen tinted; we would have to rely on our silversuits to keep us cool. 'We won't be going in as far as last time, Bob – the nearest pride of lions I know of is on the border between zones blue and orange. But set against that, we'll probably be out there for longer, depending on how fast we can bag a lion.' He peered ahead, his face beaded with sweat.

The still, lifeless foreshore of the fire zone approached, and the truck made the transition from sea to sand with hardly a jolt. I pulled on my gloves and raised my hood; the thermometer on the dash indicated that the temperature in the cab was 120°. We veered from the track we had followed the other day, heading north towards a region of ravines and canyons which split the surface on Brightside.

At this proximity the light show strung out between Main Island in the south and the Solar Research building was spectacular. Although the actual building was way to our left and out of sight, the great golden bolts of illumination showed as foreshortened blasts of fire, igniting the area around the station in blinding sunbursts.

The Telemass activity recalled to mind my trip to Main.

I mentioned to Abe that I'd seen Doug Foulds yesterday.

He glanced across at me. 'And?'

'Well, he thinks he knows who the uniform belonged to.'

Abe laughed. 'So he's willing now to admit that we did see a body?'

'Let's just say that he's keeping an open mind. The suit belonged to a woman who worked at the station, and she just happens to have gone missing on a boating trip recently.'

'Who was she?'

'Director Steiner's deputy, a woman called Hannah Rodriguez.'

'Rodriguez?'

I looked at him. 'You know her?'

'We met last year. She spent a lot of time at Trevellion's.'

I nodded. 'Doug told me. He asked me if I'd ask Fire about her and Trevellion.'

'He doesn't think—?'

I laughed. 'That's what I asked him. I don't think he has a clue what's going on at the moment.'

'Has he questioned Steiner about her?'

'I'm not sure. I presume so.'

'He should have found out a lot from him, if Steiner was willing to open up, that is. He and Rodriguez had differences of opinion as to how the station should be run. Rodriguez spent a lot of time with Trevellion on the island, and more than once I heard her complain about Steiner.'

We fell silent, each to our own thoughts.

We hovered at an even hundred kilometres per hour towards zone orange, drawing a great spume of sand in our wake. The temperature in the cab rose steadily — at a 160° I drank a litre of water from the canteen and lowered the face-mask, but all that achieved was to block out the glare; the heat was intolerable.

We passed rafts of low-lying vegetation — paddle-shaped cacti with bright pink flowers. I felt a familiar surge of delight at the sight, quickly followed by the realization that the days of my frost dependency were, hopefully, behind me; then I realized that the sickness and nausea I had experienced all morning had passed. I was hot, sticky and uncomfortable, but no longer ill. I thought back to that morning, and felt relief and pride that I'd had the strength to turn my back on the frost in the half-shell. For the next hour, in a bid to take my mind off the merciless heat, I considered Fire and where we might go gliding.

As we left zone blue, the terrain this far north changed. A fissure cracked the parched sand of the desert beside us, opened up into a rift valley perhaps twenty kilometres long, five wide and one deep. In the narrow valley bottom, away from the direct light of the sun, I made out the gnarled trickle of a meagre stream, flanked by patches of tropical greenery.

'It's an underground spring,' Abe said, noticing my interest. 'It irrigates the valleys and makes them havens for wildlife. We're not far off the lions' breeding ground. They gather here every cycle, mate and have their young, then move inland, scavenging. There should still be a few stragglers around. They breed once a year, and it was just over a year since I was last here.'

We came to a second, smaller canyon, parallel to the first. Abe stopped the truck and we admired the view. From here to the coast, the land was scarred and chapped with a series of steaming vents and fissures. Before us, the desert dropped away into a wide canyon. A rainbow hung half-way down the far incline, in the mist created by the perfect arc of a waterfall. The valley bottom was a tangle of jungle, patched with cloud. I had never imagined that such a place existed on Brightside.

'Good God, it's beautiful . . .'

Abe smiled. 'The Cunningham Rift,' he said.

'You discovered it?' I asked, surprised.

He laughed. 'No – the original exploration team discovered it, gave it a number.'

'Then how come . . . ?'

'It's named after my wife, Pat,' Abe said. 'She lost her life here last year.'

I stared at him. He quickly lowered his face-mask. 'We're wasting time, Bob. Let's get to it.'

He unclipped a laser from the rack, opened the door and jumped out. He strode to the edge of the escarpment and surveyed the terrain below. I joined him.

He indicated a boulder among the scree five metres down the slope. We slid down, grabbing at each other for support and creating a minor avalanche of sand and rock, the sound clattering and echoing in the stillness.

We reached the cover of the boulder and Abe rested his rifle on its apex like the last defender of some old-time stockade. I was panting from the exertion; we might have been fifty kilometres nearer the coast than we were on our last trip, but the increased activity of the solar flares made the difference negligible.

'The lions keep to the valley bottom during mating periods,' Abe said. 'As soon as I see a likely candidate, I want you to return to the truck and take it over the edge. I'll pot the lion, jump aboard and we'll make straight for it before it has time to come round.'

I nodded, staring down the slope at the distant jungle. I made out the occasional pterosaur, flapping through the tree-tops, but there was no sign of any lions.

Beside me, Abe clutched his rifle and cursed whenever a movement in the valley bottom turned out to be something other than a lion. I had never seen him this tense before; he was far from his usual composed self, and it struck me that his eagerness to bag a lion was at odds with the Abe I knew, the conservationist who had turned his island into a sanctuary for the endangered species of the planet.

I broke my silence. 'Abe, I appreciate this.'

He glanced across at me. I made out a faint smile beneath his tinted face-mask. 'Don't mention it.'

'You don't mind . . . ?' I gestured.

He shook his head. 'I've been thinking about it ever since Trevellion asked me to capture her a lion at the party the other night. I didn't want to do it then, for *her*, but . . . I have to admit that I regretted turning down her offer. Over the past two days the thought's never been far from my mind – I've even dreamed about it.' He returned his scrutiny to the rift valley.

I shrugged. 'I just thought you might object to what Trevellion's going to do with it.'

'I suppose part of me does, Bob. But some other, infantile side of me relishes the prospect.'

I stared at him.

'I need to lay the ghost, get my revenge. I know it's stupid, unworthy of me . . .'

'Revenge?' I echoed.

'Revenge, Bob, for what happened here a year ago. Didn't you know? Pat was attacked and killed by a sand lion.'

87

Despite the heat, I began to shiver as if with shock. 'Christ, Abe. If I'd known . . . I'm sorry. I should never have asked you.'

He laughed. 'Bob, I told you. I need this. Perhaps something good will come of it—'

He stopped. His body tensed, and he stared down the valley at a hunched, shambling form emerging from the undergrowth and rooting through the sand with its horned snout. At the sight of the beast, I was overcome by its power and air of menace.

'Get the truck down here!' Abe hissed.

I ran back up the slope, slipping and sliding as I went. Seconds before I reached the vehicle, I heard the quick hiss of laser fire followed by a bone-jarring clunk as the bolt connected with the armoured lion. I dived into the cab and eased the truck over the edge of the precipice, my chest hitting the wheel as I took the slope, turbos roaring. Abe was standing on the boulder, and as I passed he leapt on to the flat-bed and readied the crane mechanism.

Two hundred metres below us, the sand lion lay on its side, stumpy legs twitching. Its mouth hung open, revealing an awry thicket of sickle-shaped fangs, and its thick brow-ridge was scorched from the impact of the laser.

I slowed the truck and drew alongside, keeping the turbos running for a quick retreat should the animal recover. In the flat-bed Abe was working frantically to hoist the cage on its boom and swing it over the side. As I waited, wondering how soon the lion might come to its senses and seek revenge, the barred shadow of the cage swooped over the cab and out above the lion. Abe lowered the cage – it contained the animal with just centimetres to spare – then activated the bars in the base. They displaced the lion, rolling it on to its back, and snapped into place. He hit the switch to retrieve the cage, and the crane mechanism groaned and the truck yawed on its cushion of air as the cage bearing the one tonne of armoured meat lifted and swung by agonizing degrees back over the cab and on to the flat-bed. The cage hit the deck and the truck bucked.

I was about to rev the turbos, turn and head for the slope when the second lion emerged at a gallop from an arbour of vines and lianas. It paused long enough to allow its tiny brain to assess the situation, then decided that the truck could be considered a predator and charged.

'Abe!' I cried. It was the first and last thing I could do before the lion smashed head on into the front fender. The jarring impact sent the truck into a careering backspin. I wrestled with the controls, the turbos whining with the strain of maintaining balance and height with so heavy a cargo aboard.

The vehicle stabilized, facing the stunned lion. It gained its feet, and only when I realized that it was intent on a second charge did I see Abe. The impact had pitched him from the flat-bed; he was on his hands and knees, mid-way between the truck and the animal. The lion charged, the truck forgotten for more edible prey.

I accelerated, stuck my head through the open window and yelled, 'Abe!'

He had the presence of mind to fall flat as the truck swept over him and crashed into the advancing lion. This time the lion hit with a crunch of bone, the fender sprang loose and the hood buckled. I winded myself against the wheel and the truck swung away to reveal Abe on his belly a matter of feet away from the stunned lion, already stirring itself. I accelerated again, swung open the passenger door and yelled at him to get inside. Dazed, he staggered to his feet and launched himself into the cab as the lion charged and smashed the door shut behind him. I opened the throttle and headed for the incline, and Abe collapsed into the seat and laughed with shock and relief.

Once out of the ravine and on the flat plain of Brightside, I cut the turbos. The truck settled; the cooling engine ticked in the silence. The caged lion was still unconscious.

'Christ, Abe . . .'

He regarded me, laughed. 'I'm fine, Bob. I owe you one. You never told me you were a demolition derby champion.'

I smiled. 'I wasn't,' I said. 'I just crashed smallships.'

Abe took a long drink from the canteen and passed it to me. We exchanged seats and he drove away from the Cunningham Rift, on a course parallel to the ocean.

'Have I ever told you what happened back there last year?' he asked after a while. He went on before I could reply, 'We'd been watching lions for a couple of years before we traced them to the rift, and when we found their breeding ground we decided to film them. We could have installed remote cameras in the valley bottom, but I wanted to go one better. Can you imagine that?'

'You went down there and filmed them yourselves?'

'We planned to go into the valley, knock out a lion and fit it with a camera, linked to home. We'd done it with smaller animals, but nothing as big or as dangerous as a lion. We knew a well-aimed laser could put it under long enough for us to strap a miniature camera to its skull. It should have been a quick, routine operation . . .'

In the cage behind us, the lion roared. I looked through the rear window, and the sight of the angry armour-plated beast, with only a metre between us, made me uneasy. As I watched, the lion gained its feet and lunged. The truck side-swiped, and Abe fought to get it back on course.

'Anyway,' he continued, 'we went into the valley with the truck – this truck – and a couple of lasers, parked up and waited. It wasn't long before a lion showed itself, poking around the truck. I waited until it was retreating, fired and hit the side of its head. It went down instantly and didn't stir.'

He stopped here, gripping the wheel. 'We climbed out and approached the lion. Pat had the camera. She stood by its head and positioned the camera at the base of its frontal horns. I fastened the straps. We were working fast. We reckoned we had about forty-five seconds, sixty tops . . . We reckoned wrong. The lion came to and struggled to its feet. We ran, but the lion was between Pat and the truck. She tried to circle round it and get back to the truck . . . but the lion cut her off and lunged. The stupid thing was, Bob, I'd left my laser in the cab. I had to run back for it while the lion . . . while it attacked Pat. I emptied a dozen bolts into it, probably concussed it for days. Then I picked Pat up and carried her back to the truck. Christ, she was in a bad way . . . but I thought that if I got her to Main fast enough – the marvel of modern medicine and all that.' He opened his palms flat on the wheel, closed them and shook his head. 'It was no good, Bob. I got there a couple of hours later and the surgeons started work on her straight away, but it was no good. There was nothing they could do.' He gave a sudden bitter laugh. 'From that day, I've kept away from the lions. I blamed myself for not taking a laser with me. Perhaps if I had . . .' He looked at me and smiled. 'We can play "what if" for ever, Bob, but it doesn't change a thing.'

He lapsed into silence then, and for the next thirty minutes we travelled on without a word. Only the lion gave voice, roaring in protest at its continued captivity and lurching from side to side in the cage.

The Solar Research Station emerged from the heat haze on the horizon, a ziggurat of blinding white blocks with sloping, darkened windows. Beside it, I made out what I thought was a second, smaller building – though I could not recall having seen it there before. The Telemass operation had ceased.

Abe drove through the gates and into the compound. He settled the truck before the building, opened the door and jumped out. He stopped, then. He stared back between the truck and the façade of the station, his expression watchful.

'Abe?' I asked.

He glanced back at me. 'Stay where you are,' he said. 'Get down!'

I moved fast, slipped from the seat and curled in the footwell. Abe slammed the door.

'Hey!' someone called. The cry echoed off the front of the building, accompanied by the sound of footsteps.

All I could see from my foetal position was the top of Abe's head. Seconds later he was joined by someone wearing a light-blue Telemass cap and carrying a laser rifle: its barrel projected over his shoulder.

'What the hell . . . ?' the Telemass guard said.

'I was just passing. I saw the lights. Abe Cunningham – zoologist.'

'I'm afraid I'll have to ask you to accompany me, Mr Cunningham.'

They moved off, their footsteps receding.

I was torn between remaining where I was and leaping out and following Abe. But Abe's warning, and the sight of the armed guard, spoke to the coward in me. I stayed where I was, curled uncomfortably beneath the dash.

Minutes passed before I began to question the ridiculousness of my reactions. I had no reason to assume that Abe was in danger. Telemass guards with lasers were, after all, a common sight on Main.

I decided to find out what was keeping Abe. I sat up, opened the door and jumped out, and as I did so the area around the station was bathed in an explosion of golden light as quick as lightning.

Cautiously I walked away from the truck, rounded the corner of the station and came upon what earlier I had assumed was a second building. Now I saw it was nothing of the sort. Stacked in the compound beside the Research Station were a dozen long industrial containers – a monolithic unit silhouetted against the bright horizon.

Of Abe and the guard, or anyone else, there was no sign.

Behind the building, the Telemass Organization had set up a small hexagonal pad of bronze metal, perhaps fifty metres across. Beside it was a control tower, identical to the one at the station on Main, but in miniature. An air of stillness and desertion, at one with the abandoned atmosphere of the rest of the station, hung over the Telemass apparatus.

I retraced my footsteps to the stack of containers. Across the corrugated surface of the first was stencilled: B26a/Hydroponics/ Meridian/Beta Hydri VI. I moved on to the next and read: B26b/ Harvester/Meridian/Beta Hydri VI.

I wondered why such supplies had been designated to Meridian, and why the Telemass Organization thought it necessary to stockpile the supplies out here in the middle of nowhere. Then I recalled the flash of golden light, and wondered why they had 'massed Abe back to Main Island . . .

I returned to the truck, drove out of the compound and back towards the sea, feeling not so much uneasy as confused. The frantic activity of the caged lion ensured that I kept my mind on the driving. One hour later I came upon the welcome sight of the ocean, and thirty minutes after that I settled the truck on the jetty of my island.

I lost no time in contacting the Telemass station. I demanded to be put through to Director Wolfe Steiner – but the receptionist told me that the Director was busy and could talk to no one.

I calmed myself with the thought that I was getting worked up over nothing, that Abe had probably been detained for trespassing on what was now Telemass Organization property. There was nothing to worry about, I told myself. I decided against calling Doug Foulds and asking his advice. No doubt Abe would call me when he got the chance.

I recalled the sand lion on the back of the truck. I showered, changed, and then made my way to Trevellion's island.

I gunned the engine of the truck, surged from the marina and made my way along a narrow track which curved around the bay and climbed gently towards the hilltop dome. The sand lion ceased its roaring and contented itself with gnawing the bars of its cage.

I arrived on the lawn where the party had been held, settled the truck and jumped down. Off to one side, a dozen workmen were putting the finishing touches to a long caged run: the sand lion's home away from home. A battery of lamps was directed at the enclosure to provide the animal with the heat and light of Brightside.

Tamara Trevellion, her scales flashing a petroleum sheen in the sunlight, supervised the operation. She moved from man to man, giving advice and instruction with her usual air of disdain. I looked around for Fire.

Trevellion turned, saw me, and stepped across the lawn, fins rippling in the breeze of her advance. Her piscean expression, heavy and deadpan, was an unreadable as ever. 'Benedict,' she called. 'I trust the animal caused you no trouble?'

The workmen had inserted a grav-sled beneath the cage and were in the process of ferrying it across the lawn to the run. We stood side by side and watched the operation.

Before we'd set off to Brightside, Abe located a disc of information he'd compiled about sand lions. 'Abe Cunningham came with me. He sent you this.' I held out the disc. 'A few hints on how to keep the lion.'

'I've made the requisite studies already, of course. But thank Cunningham anyway, won't you?'

I nodded, at a loss, the disc extended like a hand to be shaken. I returned it to my pocket. 'Is Fire here?' I asked.

'She is presently at her studies, but she will be finished shortly.'

'I'd like to see her about tomorrow. That is' – I glanced at the fish-woman – 'if she can still accompany me.'

Trevellion turned on me what I interpreted to be a cold glare – though all her looks, with eyes that rarely blinked, could be described as cold and glaring. 'I am a woman of my word, Benedict. Of course she can still accompany you.'

We lapsed into silence and watched the workmen lower the cage into the run. They threw a switch on the cage and the sand lion bounded out, charged the length of the run and attacked the bars when it realized that its freedom was illusory. The structure shuddered under the barrage. The animal gave off an acrid, putrescent reek and, even though it was caged, its primal ferocity filled me with fear.

Trevellion turned to me. 'Would you care for a refreshment, Benedict?' Without awaiting my reply she swept off across the lawn towards the dome. I followed her, glad to get away from the lion. I had visions of it escaping the cage and savaging everyone on the island. Not for the first time I wondered if her surgeon's expertise would be sufficient to quell and control the beast.

I stepped into the sunken lounge which comprised a sectioned-off quarter of the dome. The two interior walls were hung with works of art signed, I found on closer inspection, in Tamara's flamboyant script. They were montages of crystals and gemstones, to my untutored eye quite beautiful.

'Early work of no great merit,' Trevellion called from across the room. 'Would you care for an imported brandy?'

I said that I'd prefer a fruit juice, incurring her displeasure. She passed me the glass and, rather than remain beside her and attempt conversation, I moved around the room, inspecting the other works. They were displayed on pedestals, sculptures in every medium imaginable from crystal to wood, gold to diamond. It struck me that those signed by Tamara, as opposed to the creations of Maximilian Trevellion, were not as accomplished. I recalled that Tamara had only really been recognized as an original artist with her live events after the death of her husband.

Trevellion stood at the centre of the room, poised elegantly beside a triangular crystal sculpture. She took delicate sips from a monstrous balloon glass. 'I practised in every medium during the years of my apprenticeship, Benedict. I found the permanence of those works appealing – though at the same time I was dissatisfied. What is the advantage of a permanent record of an inferior work of art?'

I demurred. 'I don't know . . . these seem very good to me.'

Trevellion said frostily, 'You are right, Benedict. You do not know. These pieces are crass and vulgar. I keep them on show to remind me of my failure – to spur me on to produce an even greater work. When the ultimate event is achieved, I shall take great delight in personally destroying every last one of these . . . these *objects*.'

'You seem to be achieving acclaim with your events,' I said.

Leisurely, she took a sip of brandy. 'I have always been a poet, and my most recent poetry is my best work to date. By combining evocative words and complimentary visualizations, one can achieve much more than these static works. Until now, however, I have never given a thought to recording and editing these events for posterity – or rather I have, but the technical difficulties of such an undertaking have always rather deterred me. I have been working on these difficulties of late, and my next event will be taped, and then edited. The event, by the way, will be held three days from now. You are invited.'

Somewhat surprised, I thanked her. I wondered at her sudden hospitality, so soon after warning me away from not only the island but also her daughter.

'I'll look forward to it,' I said.

She inclined her head. 'It should be quite a spectacular show.'

It seemed we had reached an impasse. Trevellion had invited me in to ask me to her forthcoming event, and I had gratefully accepted. Now I felt uncomfortable. No doubt any further observations by me as regards her art would be greeted with disdain, and Trevellion was not a woman to indulge in idle smalltalk. I hastily finished my drink, wondering if I dare ask after her daughter again.

In the event I was saved the bother.

Fire, radiant in silver lamé dungarees, appeared in the archway leading to the rest of the dome. 'Mr Benedict! What are you—' For the second before she caught sight of her mother, she was the vital Fire I knew; then, as Trevellion stepped out from behind the crystal that had partially hidden her, Fire faltered and stared at her mother with wide eyes, as if the exhibition of normal youthful exuberance was sufficient to earn her a reprimand.

'Oh, I'm sorry. I didn't see you—'

'I do not tolerate interruptions, Fire. Do you presume for a second that I would leave a guest alone to his own devices? Benedict and I were discussing my work. I suggest that you go outside until we have finished.'

The command was delivered in a monotone which brooked no

dissent. Fire, without so much as a glance my way, hurried through the lounge and outside. I watched her cross the lawn and climb the hillock which overlooked the dome, hands in pockets, head down.

'Allow me to apologize for my daughter's behaviour, Benedict—'

'Fire's behaviour?' I shook my head. 'She did nothing wrong . . .'

It seemed then that amusement played on her thin, aquatic lips. 'Fire is a wayward child. I see in her many aspects of myself when I was her age – aspects which I do not particularly like.'

I was incensed. 'How do you expect her to grow as a person, develop her own character, if you keep her imprisoned here and treat her like that? Have you ever considered that she might improve in your eyes if you allowed her a little freedom?'

'I think I have explained the situation to you before,' Trevellion said.

I could have left it there, gone out and joined Fire. But Trevellion's arrogance infuriated me. 'I think I understand why you treat her as you do,' I began.

She turned on me. 'You understand *nothing*!'

'You should put your past behind you,' I went on. 'Forget the tragedy and Fire's part in it and learn to accept her.'

'That is impossible, Benedict.'

I walked across the lounge and stared out through the clear curving wall of the dome. Fire sat cross-legged on the summit of the hillock with her back to us. I turned to face Trevellion, who was leaning against a pedestal, regarding me.

'I would have thought that an artist of your calibre and sensitivity would be able to manage their personal affairs better than you do.'

Trevellion threw back her head and laughed. 'You are clearly no artist, Benedict. Do you think that because we attempt to create perfection our lives are likewise perfect? Think again! We create art out of chaos, we try to make sense of the travesty of our existence. My personal life and relationships are no longer important as such, what does matter is my work. My art feeds off my neurosis. Without this, there would be no art.'

I looked at the objects set on the plinths and pedestals around the room. I gestured. 'But these are objects of beauty,' I said. 'Not—' I had been about to say 'not madness', but stopped myself.

Trevellion made a dismissive, sweeping gesture. 'These are old and imperfect. My more recent creations are what matter.' She paused, and cast me what might have been a calculating look. 'But if you don't believe me, attend my next event.'

I nodded. 'I'll do that,' I said, bitterly.

Trevellion finished her drink. 'I suggest you go and join Fire, she's awaiting you. But before you go,' she went on, 'I'd like to ask you one question: do you love my daughter, Benedict?'

I paused by the exit, turned and looked back at the fish-woman, considering the question. 'I admire her bravery,' I said, 'her resilience. Many others would have cracked under the strain of the regime you impose on her.' I shrugged. 'Perhaps . . .'

'Yes?' Her gelid eyes regarded me impassively.

'Perhaps I feel sorry for her,' I said. 'But that doesn't mean that I don't feel affection as well.'

Trevellion regarded me with a gaze so cold I was suddenly unnerved, and then turned to replenish her glass.

I hurried from the dome, crossed the lawn and climbed the hill towards the seated figure of Fire. She was contemplating the broad sweep of the ocean without really seeing a thing, her palms upturned in the bowl of her crossed legs.

I dropped down tiredly beside her.

She smiled. 'I was thinking about going gliding with you,' she said. 'I was wondering what the island would look like from the air.' Her eyes widened in sudden alarm. 'I can still go, can't I?'

'I delivered my part of the bargain,' I said. 'I'll pick you up tomorrow at first light.'

'I just thought that . . . maybe Tamara had changed her mind. I wouldn't put it past her, especially after . . . What was she talking to you about?' she asked brightly.

'Her art,' I said. 'You. I think I angered her. I told her that I didn't like the way she treated you.'

She stared at me. 'You didn't?'

'I couldn't stand by and say nothing.'

Fire shrugged. 'I no longer notice that much.' She was staring at her hands as she said this, and I wondered if it was the truth. I guessed that her show of stoic unconcern was just her way of bearing up.

'Your life must have been hell since the accident,' I said.

'The accident?' Mystification showed in her eyes like a flaw in a jewel.

'The death of your father,' I said. 'The reason your mother . . .'

Fire made a sound like a short laugh of despair, or helplessness, at the thought of my ignorance. 'It wasn't exactly heaven when he was alive. Tamara hated me long before the accident – but back then I think she didn't really know why. She didn't have an excuse.' She lapsed into a silence more profound because it was obvious that she wanted to confide in me.

'In a way,' she murmured, 'it was even worse before the accident. Tamara hated me, and of course I had no idea why. I understood only later.'

She lifted her shoulders in an exaggerated where-to-begin shrug. 'Tamara wasn't successful when Max was alive,' she said. 'Oh, she made a living, her poetry was popular, but she was forever in his shadow. She tried hard, but nothing ever really worked out to her satisfaction. She was never acclaimed as the great artist she wanted to be. There's no one as self-destructive as an unsuccessful artist, Bob. She hated herself, but her ego wouldn't allow that. For a time she turned that feeling on Max, resented his success. Then Jade came along, and then me – as if we'd been ordered into existence for the very reason that Tamara needed others beside herself to hate. I honestly can't remember the early years. They're just a blur. I just remember being very unhappy and not understanding why my mother treated me like she did. My father was no help, either. He was too wrapped up in his own work. He hardly noticed me. Then Max died, and suddenly Tamara had a reason for hating me. It came as a kind of relief, I suppose. I could almost accept it. You see, although she resented Max, she also loved him. I lived in his place and she had a legitimate reason for hating me.

'It's ironic – since Max's death, Tamara's achieved her first real success as an artist. The really sad thing is because it came only after his death, she resents the success and hates herself even more for not achieving it while he was alive. She's a mess, Bob. But I wish she didn't have to take it out on me.'

As I listened to her, I looked across the island to the upsweeping face of the next valley. It was the glade I had visited the other evening with Fire. I thought of Jade Trevellion and her death.

'Did Tamara treat Jade like she treats you?' I asked now.

Fire nodded. 'We found strength in each other. We disliked Tamara, and that made us all the closer. I don't know if I realized this at the time, or understood only later, when I came to understand why Tamara hated us so much.'

'Do you think Jade understood why Tamara felt like this?'

Fire frowned in concentration. 'She never said anything to me . . . But she was my age, old enough to understand people's motives.' Fire paused, then looked up at me. 'Of course she must have understood Tamara. Towards the end, Jade was sympathetic towards her, often defending her. It angered me. I didn't understand. In her last year, Jade began working with Tamara on several projects. It seems strange that Tamara would allow Jade to assist in her creations. I remember that I felt betrayed at the time. They were working together when the accident happened . . .' She stopped there, as if reluctant to go on.

I lay back on the grass and stared into the sky. The slow advance of the shield was bringing a roseate twilight to the island. We watched pterosaurs migrate *en masse* towards Brightside.

I changed the subject. 'Tomorrow we'll take the glider up to Main,' I said. 'We could go to the museum and see the sculpture, if you like. Then you have an appointment with the neurospecialist in the afternoon.'

'Bob . . .'

'You did agree,' I reminded her.

She nodded. 'I know. But it's just that . . .' She shrugged. 'The thought of defying Tamara . . .'

'Hey.' I propped myself up on one elbow and took her hand. 'There's no way Tamara will find out, OK? As far as she'll know, we'll be gliding.'

She still looked uncertain. 'But what if the surgeon *can* treat me? Tamara's surgeon will find out for sure, and then—'

'Then you'll have the perfect opportunity to get away from here,' I said.

She nodded, but nevertheless looked distinctly uncomfortable.

We watched the shield occlude the sun, the shadow sweep across the ocean towards the island. The Brightside horizon burned like banked, flickering coals. Fire sat beside me, and as I regarded her I saw a glint of silver at the back of her head, beneath strands of long blonde hair. Wordlessly I drew her to me – she stiffened a little, thinking my move an advance – and before she could protest I parted her hair to reveal a console, a tiny strip set flush with her skull.

She turned, her hand touching the back of her head. 'I'm not Augmented, Bob,' she protested.

I laughed. 'Does it matter? Here—' I took her hand and directed it to my occipital console. 'A sub-cortical,' I said, 'with chips in a dozen areas of my brain. I used it when I was a pilot to integrate with my ship.'

'This is so the surgeon can monitor my condition,' Fire told me, touching her own implant. 'He just interfaces and sees how I'm doing.'

'How long have you been ill?' I asked.

She shrugged. 'So long that I don't remember. Years. I had this installed soon after the tumour was diagnosed.' She seemed reluctant to continue. 'Please, Bob.'

Darkness had descended and the stars were out above Darkside. We sat in silence for a while and stared at the diamond-hard points of brightness.

I remembered what Doug had requested the other day. 'By the way,' I said, taking the pix from the inside pocket of my jacket. 'Do you recognize her?'

She took it and frowned. 'It's Hannah Rodriguez.'

'Did you know her well?'

'No, not at all. She's a friend of Tamara's.'

'Were they close?'

'I don't really know.' She pushed out her lips. 'Reasonably, I suppose. She spends a lot of time here. I haven't seen her for a while though.'

'Has Tamara mentioned her at all recently?'

'I don't know.' She hunched her shoulders again. 'Why the interest?'

I hesitated. 'She's been missing for a while,' I said.

'Missing?' She looked alarmed. 'What do you mean . . . *missing*?'

'Well, Abe and I found the remains of her uniform on Brightside a few days ago. Doug Foulds thinks someone might have . . .'

She was staring into space, shaking her head.

'Fire?'

She frowned at me. 'It's strange. Rodriguez spent so much of her time around here, I feel I should remember her more than I do. The thing is, I can't recall talking to her on one single occasion. But I know I must have, at some time.' She looked up at me. 'That's the worst thing about my illness, Bob. Not the pain, but the fact that chunks of my past are just . . . *gone*.'

We stared at the stars in silence, hand in hand, before Tamara emerged from the dome at the foot of the hill and called Fire's name.

She quickly released my hand. 'That's Tamara.' We climbed to our feet. 'I'll see you tomorrow, OK?'

She almost skipped down the hill to the dome.

I made my way to the truck on the lawn.

I was half-way up the path to my dome when I heard the urgent buzzing of the vid-screen. I ran the rest of the way, expecting the caller to hang up just as I entered the lounge. I stabbed the *accept* button and flopped into the chair, exhausted.

The wall screen flickered and flared into life. Abe stared out at me. He still wore his silversuit. His long grey hair was dishevelled and he needed a shave.

'Bob – I thought you'd never answer.'

'Abe, where the hell are you?' I stared at him. 'What's wrong?'

'I'm in the Meridian Star Hotel. I'm staying here for a while. I think it's safer than returning to my villa.'

'Abe, what's going on—?'

He pinched the bridge of his nose, as if in thought. His hand was shaking. He looked up. 'They arrested me at the station and Telemassed me back to Main. Steiner questioned me. I asked him about the containers. He told me . . .'

I stared at him. 'What?'

Abe looked devastated. 'He took me outside his office, explained that he thought it was bugged. Then he told me everything. He warned me that if his adviser got to know that I knew . . .' Abe shrugged. 'He intimated that if Weller got to know, then he couldn't guarantee my safety.'

'What did he tell you, Abe?'

He stared out at me, something terrible in his expression. 'Look, Bob . . . I'll be down to see you soon. I'll tell you everything then.'

'I'll be in Main tomorrow,' I said. 'We could meet.'

He looked into my eyes. 'It might be best if I didn't involve you further.'

'Christ, Abe. I want to know!' I could see from his expression that he needed to talk.

He just stared out at me, as if deciding the wisest course of action. 'Very well. Where will you be?'

'The Museum of Modern Art. I'll meet you in the foyer, around one?'

He tried his best to smile. 'I'll see you then.' He cut the connection.

I sat and stared at the blank screen, trying to make sense of what Abe had just told me. Whether in reaction to this, or because the symptoms of withdrawal had reached their cyclic high point again, I was feeling terrible. My limbs were jumping, and the pain in the pit of my stomach was counterpointed by a pulsing, stabbing sensation at the base of my skull. I had no idea if withdrawal from frost had ever killed anyone, but right now I felt close to death.

I moved to the chesterfield and sat down. The half-shell was before me on the coffee table. I picked it up, held it unsteadily in my lap. Certain granules in the pile of pink powder coruscated like diamond filings. I inhaled, relishing the sickly sweet stench of the raw drug. All I had to do was to pinch a line, lay it on the copper plate of the burner, ignite it and inhale . . . For eight or more hours I would be oblivious of everything – Abe's situation, Fire's dilemma, the pain that wracked my body – and in the morning I would feel much better, cured of the sickness.

Then the rational part of me took control again. I stumbled from the lounge, locked myself in my room and spent a sleepless night.

6

NEMESIS

As seen from the altitude of more than a kilometre, the meridian sea and the archipelago slung along its broad blue bow was reduced to one vast perspective, observable in its entirety. Likewise the dramas and incidents enacted beneath the domes of the many islands were reduced, made insignificant. For the past week I had been part of so many happenings that at times I had found it difficult to make sense of anything: Trevellion's treatment of her daughter, Fire's illness, the remains we had discovered and, after Abe's communication last night, Director Steiner's obvious involvement... Although it occurred to me that the events were connected, I was unable to discern an overall pattern. The act of removing myself from the surface of the planet did not grant me the answer in one mighty transcendent flash, or allow me to view the series of incidents in one clear mosaic of linked circumstance, but I did suddenly see what was important to me in the morass of mystery and confusion. I was setting out now on a course of action which would hopefully bring about Fire Trevellion's liberation from the influence of her mother. I wished I was as confident about how I might help Abe.

I lay horizontal in the thermal sling beneath the yellow sun-reflective wing, the engine a perpetual drone in my ears. I cast my eye over the scatter of small islands stretching into the distance. The island immediately beneath me, dotted with a dozen silver domes, was Abe's. I passed over it in less than a second and continued out across the sun-flecked sea. When Trevellion's island loomed below, more prominent than those before and after it, I banked and made a slow, lazy spiral down to the beach where I had arranged to meet

Fire. I slipped from the sling and came to rest gently in the sand, the wing angled above me like a canopy.

There was no sign of Fire, but it was still early. I had set off even before the trailing edge of the shield had revealed the sun. Only now did the full light of Beta Hydri burn across the wastes of Brightside, dissipating the humidity from the air and heating the sand.

I remained in the harness for a few minutes, exhausted. The good thing was that I felt no worse today than I had at the same time yesterday; I hoped that the symptoms of withdrawal were beginning to ease up. Certainly, if the bouts of sweating and shaking and the accompanying nausea became any worse, then I was not sure of my resolve to steer clear of frost. I began to wish that I'd been determined enough to dispose of my supplies of the drug before now – but the coward in me had shied at the thought of cutting the connection with the insular and withdrawn life I had led until now.

I climbed from the frame, strode up the beach and sat on a rock facing the sea. I was more than a little apprehensive, not so much at the prospect of gliding all the way to Main with a passenger, which I had never done before, but at what was to follow. Later today I would find out precisely the extent of Fire's illness, and whether or not there was an effective and inexpensive cure. There was always, of course, the chance that Trevellion and her surgeon were truthful in their claim that Fire's condition was expensive to treat. It was this that I feared and, perhaps, the thought that her mother had kept something from her, that the illness was in fact worse than she had told Fire.

Thirty minutes later there was still no sign of her. It occurred to me that Trevellion might have had second thoughts about allowing Fire to go gliding, after my criticism of her yesterday.

I was about to make my way across the sand when I saw the burly figure of a security guard at the foot of the path up the hillside. He was standing with one foot lodged on the low concrete wall, an arm resting on his knee. His attitude, at once negligent and hostile, suggested that he had been watching me at his leisure for some time.

He made an imperious, beckoning gesture, then returned his hand to the butt of his holstered fire-arm. I approached, and his unremitting stare brought me out in a hot sweat.

'Trevellion,' he reported, without altering his stance, 'suggests you take your bird and fly back to wherever you came from.'

I held my ground. 'I came to see Fire,' I said.

He shook his head. 'No way, pal. The kid doesn't want to see you.'

His words sent a chill down my spine. 'Tell Trevellion that we have an agreement. I want to see Fire.' I took a step forward.

With an air of infinite patience the guard raised a hand, barring my way. His smile unnerved me. 'I'll tell you once again – the kid doesn't want to see you. You had your chance, and blew it.'

'Is Fire ill?'

'Hey, just climb back into your contraption, Benedict, or I'll be forced to assist you.' The use of my surname for some reason threatened me more than the way he affectionately patted his pistol.

I hesitated, considering the best course of action. There was no way I could get past the guard – but I didn't intend to meekly leave as instructed. I made my way back to the glider, strapped myself in and took off. I kept low and skirted the coastline, and when I was out of the guard's line of sight I landed in the cove where I had clandestinely moored my launch on previous visits. I left the glider propped in the sand and made my way around the headland. When I came to the beach I concealed myself behind a bush and peered out at the pathway up the hillside. The guard was slowly making his way up the incline, his back to me. I ran across the sand to the stand of vegetation which Fire had disappeared into on the evening of our first meeting. Minutes later I came across the entrance to the tunnel she had told me about, a narrow crevice between two slabs of black, volcanic rock, concealed by ferns.

I slipped into the crevice and dropped further than I had expected. I landed, knees bent, in a small, dim chamber illuminated only by a chink of sunlight from above and, faintly before me, the sparkle of silver paint daubed – evidently by Fire – along the wall to guide the way.

I gathered my breath, my pulse racing at the thought of what I was doing, and set off carefully. Arms outstretched, I stumbled along after the intermittent trail of paint. The rock underfoot was rough and uneven, and as I progressed further into the tunnel it took an upward turn, paralleling the course of the pathway above. The chink of sunlight was soon lost behind me, but the paint still sparkled up ahead. As I followed the trail, gaining confidence and speed the further I went, I thought of Fire, and the great delight she must have taken in discovering this means of escape. At regular intervals, other tunnels branched off, their mouths patches of deeper darkness in the gloom. I imagined how easy it would be to become lost, were it not for Fire's ingenuity.

After what seemed like an hour of strenuous climbing, I came to journey's end: the silver trail brightened, the gloom lightened, and the tunnel levelled out. Again I found myself in a natural chamber, a rent in the rock above me admitting a great ingot of golden sunlight. I forced my shoulders into the gap and pulled myself through into the open air. I was in the rockery of a small garden, beside a sub-dome connected to the main dome by a short corridor.

A strategically planted shrub concealed the tunnel's entrance. I crouched behind it and peered across the crescent lawn. The wall of the individual bauble was transparent, though a level of red fluid at the base of the outer and inner membranes indicated that this could be altered. A large circular bed occupied the centre of the chamber. On it, I made out Fire. She was stretched out on her back, her hands behind her head, staring up at the apex of the dome. A large book lay open beside her. She gave the impression of someone lost in reverie, or melancholy.

I had the urge to rush across the lawn, barge into the bedroom and heroically rescue her – but caution checked me. I made quite sure first that I was unobserved. The small garden was hedged in by trees and bushes, but the upper storey of the main dome overlooked Fire's chamber. So far as I could see, there was no one in the facing section of the main dome. I left the cover of the bush and ran doubled-up across the lawn to the clear, curved wall of the smaller dome.

Fire sat up at the movement. For a second she was frozen with an unrecognizable expression on her face. Then she leapt from the bed and rushed across to the circular hatch. She fumbled desperately with the catch, a look of what I took to be determination in her eyes. She stared through the hatch at me: her expression turned fearful and her fingers worked even more feverishly. On a sudden, sickening impulse, I dived against the hatch and forced it open with all my weight. Fire resisted, pushing with her shoulder and crying out aloud. She gave in suddenly, and I stumbled into the room. Fire stood facing me with determination, her exertion followed by resolve.

'Fire?'

She stared at me. 'Just go away, Mr Benedict. *Please.*'

She wore a green one-piece, the same shade as her eyes. She had pulled the sleeves down over her fists, in a gesture that struck me as both childish and belligerent.

It seemed that she was about to launch herself at me with a flurry of blows. 'Fire . . . What happened? I thought we'd agreed . . . ?'

She remained mute. I looked past her to the bed. The large book was a photograph album, opened to a pix of her sister. Beside it was the computer board from which Fire was learning her mother's poetry.

Around the dome, on tables and shelves, were dozens of personal possessions: pink elephants and pierrot dolls, pix of Earth and models of starships. I felt closer to Fire than I had at any other time before – and this made the thought of losing her all the more unbearable. It came to me that both our futures would be decided by what I said in the next few minutes. I had to be very, very careful, like someone coaxing a potential suicide away from the edge. This knowledge almost paralysed me.

'Tamara said something' – barely a whisper – 'didn't she?'

The worst possible reaction of all: silence. She just stared at me. Already, I was damned. Her eyes were red and sore from crying, and her full lips seemed more swollen than ever.

I took a leap in the dark. 'About the accident, wasn't it?'

Leaning forward, she cried, 'So it *is* true!'

In that second I felt an overwhelming surge of relief, almost triumph. I knew that it was within my ability to counter whatever malicious lies Tamara Trevellion had told her daughter; it was obvious that Fire was distraught at having to believe these lies.

'I don't know what Tamara told you, Fire,' I was speaking in a whisper, 'so I can't tell you the truth until you tell me what she said.'

Fire sniffed back a sob; then I saw why she had covered her fists with the cuffs of her one-piece – not to hit me, as I had suspected, but to wipe away her tears. She shook her head defiantly.

'Tamara was lying – whatever she told you.'

'Then you . . . you weren't responsible for the accident?'

'Is that what she told you?'

'She told me you were paid to kill all those people. She told me you were working for someone.'

I smiled, weak with relief.

'That's a lie, Fire. Can't you see – your mother doesn't want us to be together, especially after what I said to her yesterday. She doesn't want to give you any independence. Once you realize that there's a whole world out there open to you, with boundless possibilities – what's to keep you here?'

She was suspicious, hardly daring to hope. 'You had nothing to do with the accident?'

I hesitated. 'I did pilot the smallship. It should have been a smooth ride; I'd done it so many times. There had never before been an accident on the Earth–Mars run . . .'

She pursed her lips, emphasizing the point of her chin. Then, 'What happened?'

I took a breath, wondering how much to tell; I did not want to spoil the good work I'd done so far with too liberal a dose of the truth. 'We ran into an irregularity. The auto-drive was knocked out, and I had to handle the ship manually. I handled it badly. My reactions were slow, and we went down. Fifty Terran diplomats and their families died in the accident. I survived with a few others. Of course, I was responsible; it was my fault – a better pilot would have brought the ship through unscathed.'

She was shaking her head, biting her bottom lip. There was doubt in her eyes as she regarded me.

'I can't believe that Tamara would lie to me like that—'

'You can't? Christ, she's psychologically tortured you often enough in the past.'

'But this is different – there was no one else involved then!'

I almost laughed. 'Fire, your mother isn't bothered who she hurts, you or anyone else. She'll do anything to get what she wants.'

She was still regarding me with suspicion. I said, 'Can't you see – your mother's afraid of losing you. Who would she have to hate if you were to leave?'

I stopped, allowed that to sink in. Fire regarded the carpet between us, torn between obedience to her mother and loyalty to her own desires.

She said in a whisper, 'You weren't paid?'

'Of course not!'

She looked at me. 'So . . . what happened? After the accident?'

I relaxed. I was slowly winning her over. She stood before the bed, where she had backed up to in fear, but she had released her grip on her cuffs and looked at me with a new hope in her emerald eyes.

'I was hospitalized for a year—'

'But why did you come to Meridian? Why didn't you keep on piloting?'

'There was an inquiry into the accident, and of course I was found guilty of negligence. I was fired.' I shrugged. 'So I looked for somewhere warm and quiet.'

With a drug that would allow me to forget . . .

Fire stared at me, shaking her head. 'She just wanted me to hate you. She probably enjoyed seeing my reaction when she told me.'

I held out my hand.

She remained by the bed. 'I'm frightened, Bob. What if Tamara finds out?'

'I'll be with you.'

She looked at me for a long time, her gaze calculating. Then she came to a decision. She grabbed my hand.

We slipped from the dome and hurried across the lawn, then dropped through the crevice to the subterranean passage. Fire dashed ahead of me down the incline. I felt her relief, her dread at the thought that were it not for my intervention she might have blithely believed her mother's lies.

We crawled from the crevice, emerged into the sunlight and knelt beside the stand of ferns. There was no sign of the security guard, either on the beach or up the pathway. Hand in hand we ran around the cove, hugging the shrubbery at the base of the hillside, then scrambled over the headland. The glider awaited us like a giant, grounded kite.

I dragged it around to face the ocean, then programmed the engine's memory with the co-ordinates for Main Island.

Fire suddenly squeezed my arm. 'Bob, look!' She pointed to the cliff-top. On the high path which circumnavigated the island, I made out the small, dark figure of a security guard. He was strolling away from us, his hands behind his back.

Fire swept her hair from her brow, her eyes filling with tears. She could hardly contain her frantic apprehension. 'We can't go yet!' she pleaded. 'If he hears the engine and tells Tamara . . .'

'Don't worry. Get in.' I took her arm and assisted her into the thermal sling, first one foot, then the other. I pulled the zip fastener, cocooning her in the sling like a baby in a papoose.

I ducked in beside her, gripping the frame. We were all set up to go – but for the guard. He was still on the cliff-top path, but further along, mercifully still in ignorance of us.

'How long before another guard follows him?' I asked.

Fire was near to tears. 'I don't know. Not long. There's always a few patrolling the island.'

The guard had passed behind a spur of rock.

'We'll just have to risk it,' I said. 'Hold on!'

She gave a quick, terrified smile. 'I've never been up in one of these things, Bob!'

I fired the engine, ran along the beach. There was still no further sign of the guard. Our only hope that we might escape undetected was the fact that the wind was blowing from the island, carrying the splutter of the motor out to sea.

'I hope you don't mind heights, Fire!' I shouted as we lifted, the golden crescent of sand falling away beneath us.

Fire screamed into the headwind, a combination of fright, delight, and disbelief that we were finally free.

I kept the glider low, wave-hopping, so that the bulk of the island was between us and Trevellion's dome. Then we climbed steadily, the archipelago opening out beneath us.

Beside me, Fire gripped the hand-rail and stared down with wide eyes, her long blonde hair flying in the wind. 'So many islands!' she cried. 'I never knew there were so many islands!'

Silver tears streamed from her cheeks and fell into the sea.

We banked and headed for Main.

Two hours later we landed on the cliff-top greensward of the Meridian Gliding Club, stacked away the glider, and caught a cab into town. I was in two minds as to whether I should take Fire to the Museum of Modern Art. On one hand I hoped that Jade and Tamara Trevellion's collaborative work of art might exorcise the spectre of Jade that had haunted Fire for so long, release in her the knowledge of what had really happened to her sister; on the other, I feared that Fire's experience of the piece might, if it failed to act as a mnemonic, convince Fire even more that the only way to relive her sister's death was through the medium of frost.

As we hovered through the busy afternoon streets of Main, I said, 'Fire, do you really want to go to the museum?'

She turned and looked at me. 'You promised!' she said.

I shrugged. Sunlight beat in through the glass, making me uncomfortable. 'It might be more than you can take,' I said lamely.

'That's exactly what you said about frost!' she said. 'I thought we were going to the museum so that it might bring back some memories, so I don't have to use frost?'

I shrugged again, hopelessly. 'I just hope it doesn't make you want frost all the more,' I murmured.

We alighted outside the museum, a white marble building of classical Greek design, situated at the end of a long tree-lined boulevard. We climbed the steps and passed into the cool, hushed foyer. Uniformed attendants stood against the walls. Six archways gave on to as many radial galleries, works of art on pedestals and enclosed in glass diminishing in the perspective of each. At this time of day the museum was quiet. One or two people regarded sculptures and crystals with an air of solemnity, but most of the galleries were deserted. I purchased a catalogue from the sales counter, turned to the index and found: *Tamara and Jade Trevellion; Nemesis, laser sculpture, gallery six, exhibit fifty.*

We passed through the archway into the gallery. Beside me, Fire seemed subdued, as if for the first time realizing that she was about to witness the cause of her sister's death. I felt her hand slip into mine and hold on tight.

The gallery was empty of patrons, and for this I was thankful. I was conscious of what Fire must be going through, and wanted privacy when we viewed the sculpture.

We made our way down the aisle between two rows of exhibits. On one side was a display of crystals; each slab, perhaps a metre square and a centimetre thick, was canted on a stand to present a coruscating surface to the hand. Visually they were unspectacular, but to the touch they transmitted the feelings and emotions of their creators. To our left was a series of sculptures, from figurative representations of every conceivable object, to abstract designs. The materials employed ranged from wood to titanium. The base of each was labelled with the title of the piece and a brief biographical sketch of the artist.

The Trevellion sculpture occupied an alcove of its own at the very end of the gallery. We paused before it and regarded it with the aspect of pilgrims. It stood on an obsidian plinth, illuminated by an overhead spotlight – a geometric construction of silver spars, like a mechanical tarantula with its legs in the air, roughly three metres tall and shaped like a diamond. In its deactivated state, it had a certain raw power of design, the promise of greater things when the lasers were burning.

I read the engraved plate on the plinth. '*Nemesis* – Tamara and Jade Trevellion. This piece is notable for its innovative design, its intricate use of steel and lasers to produce a stunning visual harmony. Perhaps its greatest attribute is the fact that the final tragic effect was the result of mischance, as is evident when the piece is in its activated state. Tamara Trevellion is a poet and artist, and *Nemesis* is her first work to be exhibited in the museum. Jade Trevellion, her daughter, died tragically in the making of this piece.'

I read through it a second time, not at all sure that I wanted to go ahead and experience the activated work. I glanced at Fire. She was reading the notice, her lips moving slowly. She came to the end and looked at me. 'Shall I turn it on?'

I nodded and she stepped forward and chopped her hand through a bar of light on the plinth, breaking the circuit and activating the lasers.

The effect was instant and spectacular, the dazzling light-show forcing us to take a backward step in surprise and, at first, delight. From regular points along the geometric spars, bars of laser light sprang forth and criss-crossed the interior of the design, creating denser squares of colour where they intersected in an overall effect like luminous tartan.

Caught in the polychromatic vectors of the laser nexus was the ghostly image of a female figure, as insubstantial as the form of a naiad projected on to a column of smoke. Fire gasped and stared at what might have been a reflection of herself. The standing figure of Jade Trevellion looked out at us from the lattice of lasers; from time to time the image blurred, and when it refocused Jade was presented at a different angle, in a different pose, each time outfitted in a different costume. Her resemblance to Fire was remarkable and unnerving – the same long, fair hair, full lips and slanting, emerald eyes – all the more so because I recognized the clothes that Jade was wearing: the yellow trouser suit, the halter top and shorts, the silver lamé dungarees . . .

So far the images of Jade had been distant, dreamlike. Now, the scene in the network of lasers changed, became definite: Jade, standing on the greensward in a red bikini which I had never seen Fire wearing. The image gave the illusion that the girl was on the other side of the sculpture, looking through it at us. Her expression was serious, contemplative, even sad. As we watched, Jade took one step forward, then a second . . .

Then the scene shattered.

Fire was clutching me, staring at a series of fragmented images – a fleeting, anatomical montage. I made out the curve of a flank, a knee drawn up to a bare stomach, a flash of emerald eyes . . . Then the mosaic vanished, only to appear a second later in an altered configuration: I caught a glimpse of a familiar face in pain, a hand with fingers spread in agony. I drew Fire to me, tried to cover her eyes from what I sensed was coming next – but she pulled my hand away and stared into the sculpture.

We watched as the fragmented figure of Jade Trevellion in a red bikini fell forward through the cat's cradle of lasers. The expression on her face was one of frozen terror, as if in her last second of consciousness she was fully cognizant of the oblivion about to engulf her. The scalpel-sharp rays reduced her to so many units of meat. Segments of arm and leg, belly and head, tumbled through the lasers, the projection becoming ever fainter as the horror of the images increased.

Fire screamed, and I half-carried, half-dragged her from the gallery and out into the foyer. I found a secluded foam-form and sat her down, holding her to me and feeling useless as I could think of nothing to say that might ease her pain.

'Fire, Fire . . .' I closed my eyes and felt her tears soak through my shirt, as once again I saw the girl identical to Fire fall through the lethal thicket of lasers.

'The ter-terrible, terrible thing—' Fire managed at last, 'is that it tells us nothing. Whether it was an accident, or suicide . . .'

We sat for a long time, beneath a statue of the museum's benefactor, and gradually Fire's tears ceased, and she sat up and dried her eyes and tried to smile.

'Hey,' I said. 'Abe's meeting me at one. We'll go to a restaurant and have lunch, OK?'

She nodded. 'I'd like that.'

I looked up at the clock on the wall. It was after one and there was no sign of Abe in the foyer.

'Bob?' Fire said.

I smiled. 'Look – Abe told me that if he didn't make it by one, we were to go to meet him.'

We left the museum and boarded a cab. I gave our destination as the Meridian Star Hotel. Fire, quiet beside me, was too wrapped in her own thoughts to notice my apprehension. As we rushed through the bustling streets, I tried not to dwell on what Abe had told me last night.

I glanced at Fire. She saw me looking. 'It's no good, Bob,' she said in a small voice. 'I can't remember a thing. You'd think something as terrible as *that* would make me remember, wouldn't you?'

I squeezed her hand. 'These things take time,' I said, the platitude coming easily, my mind on other things.

The cab came to a halt outside a two-storey quake-safe building in the centre of town. I paid the driver and we climbed out. The day was so relentlessly normal, with the sun-browned, brightly dressed citizens of Main passing back and forth along the street, that I felt out of place, excluded from the trivial affairs of daily life by the knowledge that everything was not as it should be. I hurried Fire into the hotel and asked at the reception desk for Abe Cunningham's room number. I entered the elevator and seemed to wait an age, Fire patiently beside me, while it carried us to the second floor. The sliding door released us and I hurried along the corridor to room twenty-five. I knocked. There was no reply. My next move was to try the handle, but it struck me, absurdly, that this action would almost amount to an admission that I knew something was wrong. So I knocked again, overcome with the strange sensation that if Abe should answer I would never again bemoan any ill-luck that might befall me.

Still there was no reply.

Fire poked at the frame of the door with the toe of her moccasin. 'He might be out, Bob,' she said. She was still too far removed from what was happening to pick up on my fear.

I turned the handle and the door swung open. The room was in semi-darkness, a dilute light soaking through the drawn curtains at the far side of the small bedroom. I stepped inside, Fire behind me.

I have never considered myself superstitious, but at that moment, even though events conspired to grant me a notion of what had happened, I was loath to call Abe's name lest I should tempt fate. It struck me that my conduct now, my movements as I entered the room, might determine whether or not Abe lived. Already, I realized, I was attempting to make amends for the circumstances that had brought Abe to Main.

Because of me, Abe had ventured to Brightside . . .

Because of that, he had investigated the Solar Research Station and been arrested . . .

Abe sat upright in a chair before a desk, his back to me. Even in the twilight of the room, I could see that his head was inclined at an unnatural angle, resting on his right shoulder. His arms hung down on either side of the chair, emphasizing the fact of the unlikely posture.

A noise startled me.

Behind me, Fire was sobbing. I turned and she ran from the room. I took a step towards Abe, caught sight of the hole drilled in his temple. I closed my eyes and sat down on the bed.

I would have expected, had anyone forecast the situation before it occurred, to feel anger and rage that someone had murdered Abe, the burning desire to avenge him by killing his killer . . . But all I felt, as I sat on the corner of the bed and stared at his lifeless, hanging hand, was a cold, numb disbelief at the fact of his death. The Abe I knew was vital and alive, and death was an abstract concept that could in no way be connected to the man I had known and liked.

I left the room and took the elevator to the foyer. Fire was seated in a large padded armchair in an adjacent lounge, almost consumed by the abundant upholstery, her feet hanging inches from the floor.

I stepped into a vid-booth and got through to Doug's office. I asked to be put through to Inspector Foulds, but the receptionist informed me that he was out. I was about to report what I'd found anyway – then stopped myself. I recalled what Abe had said last night, about Director Steiner warning him that if his 'adviser', the mysterious Weller, got to know that Abe was aware of what was going on . . . I had the sudden intuition that the fewer people who knew about my connection with Abe, the better.

'Can I help you?' the receptionist asked.

I gave my home code and asked to have Doug call me as soon as possible. Then I cut the connection and collected Fire. Subdued, she took my hand as we hurried out.

I hailed a cab and gave our destination as the Meridian Institute of Medicine.

The specialist's consulting room was plush and palatial, with a thick carpet, potted ferns, and a V-shaped marble desk. Its entire south-facing wall was a clear crystal cupola, affording a spectacular view over the city. For perhaps thirty minutes I paced the length of the room, waiting for the specialist to emerge from the adjacent surgery and tell me how serious Fire's condition was.

When I walked into the oval of the cupola for perhaps the fiftieth time, I stopped and forced myself to concentrate on various aspects of the view: the vehicles in the streets, the trees lining the boulevards, the multiple windows reflecting the sun. It was as if by keeping my mind occupied I might be able to keep myself from dwelling on the events of the day. Abe's death still had about it an air of unreality, the fleeting, elusive aspect of a nightmare. I could not conceive that Abe would not be there, as large as life, when I next visited his island.

I watched a file of vehicles cross the suspension bridge to the Telemass station: juggernauts and container craft as well as smaller private cars. I recalled that, in two days from now, the last shot was due before they were rescheduled to one a month each way. I wondered if this accounted for the rush of traffic making for the station today.

I turned at a sound from the far end of the room. The door to the surgery swung open and the specialist stepped out, a small, grey-haired woman in her mid-sixties. In the room behind her, I made out an array of medical apparatus which appeared too large to be applicable to the cure of human ills: bulky body monitors and chromium frames like implements of torture.

'Mr Benedict . . .' The woman smiled. 'I'm sorry for keeping you waiting so long.'

'How bad is she?' I asked.

'We're still running tests, Mr Benedict.' She indicated a seat at the apex of the arrowhead desk, then seated herself between the arms. 'There are a few questions I'd like to ask you.' She consulted a computer screen embedded in the desk-top. 'I know this is a formality, and I'm sure we can clear it up in no time – but were you aware that Miss Trevellion has no medical record on Meridian, even though she was born here?'

I explained that Fire had been treated privately.

The specialist frowned. 'Is she dissatisfied in some way with the treatment she's been receiving?'

'Well . . . she did want a second opinion.'

'I hope you don't mind my asking, Mr Benedict – but what is your connection with the patient?'

'I . . . we're friends,' I said, and left it at that.

She smiled. 'My services are rather expensive,' she warned me. I was a normal, I was wearing my flying suit, and I cannot have presented a very convincing appearance of affluence.

I took my credit card from my wallet and passed it across the desk. The specialist accessed it, scanned the information on the screen, and returned the card without a word.

'Just one more thing. I wonder if you can tell me the name of the surgeon who was treating Miss Trevellion?'

I had heard the man's name mentioned at the party by Trevellion. 'Heathway, Hathaway – something like that. Is it important?'

'I was curious, that's all. If you'll excuse me.' She stood and made her way across the room.

I followed her. 'Do you know exactly what's wrong with Fire?' I asked.

The woman paused by the open door.

'Mr Benedict, there is actually nothing physiologically wrong with the patient.'

I smiled. 'But that's impossible.'

'Please, believe me. Fire Trevellion is as fit and healthy as you or I.' And with this she turned and entered the surgery.

As the door swung shut, I glanced through and caught a brief glimpse of Fire. She was strapped into a padded chair, itself attached to a device which resembled a gyroscope. The frame had been rotated so that she faced the floor at an angle of forty-five degrees, giving access to the back of her head. Leads and grabs hung from a swing boom overhead, and jacks were connected to Fire's occipital console. From time to time her body spasmed.

The door closed and I resumed pacing the room, considering the specialist's diagnosis and what it meant . . .

Thirty minutes later – though it seemed like hours to me – the specialist emerged with her patient. Fire moved like a somnambulist, her eyes glazed. I took her and assisted her into the seat beside mine. She found my hand.

'Fire?'

'I'm OK, Bob. I'm fine.' She spoke slowly, her words slurred.

I looked to the specialist for an explanation.

'Miss Trevellion has no illness, tumour, or brain damage whatsoever,' she said. 'She told me that so far as she was aware, the occipital console was placed there by the surgeon when she became ill, to monitor her condition. Of course, as she has no condition to monitor, this is absurd. The console is nothing more than the terminal of a module wired into her neo-cortex to facilitate the administration of certain drugs.'

My grip tightened on Fire's hand. 'What kind of drugs?'

'Does Miss Trevellion suffer specific memory loss?' the specialist asked.

Beside me, Fire nodded wordlessly, perhaps overcome by the realization of the extent of her mother's tyranny.

I said, 'Her mother's surgeon, Hathaway . . . ?'

'He administered chemical amnesiacs to suppress specific memories. I found out that much – what I don't yet know is the extent of Miss Trevellion's memory loss.'

I just stared at her. 'Is there anything you can do to help her regain those memories?'

'Ah . . . That's a difficult question to answer with any degree of certainty at this moment, Mr Benedict.' She said this with the circumspection of her profession. 'If you could bring Miss Trevellion back in two weeks—'

Fire said, 'Two weeks? Can't you see me before then?'

The specialist regarded the desk-top screen. 'I'm afraid that's impossible. I have a rather busy schedule. Even then,' she went on, 'I cannot guarantee that I would be able to restore your full memory. There will be a lot of careful exploratory work to be done before I can assess the extent of your amnesia. It might even take months.'

I nodded. 'I'll bring Fire back in a fortnight,' I said.

She went on, 'What was inflicted on Miss Trevellion was a gross breach of professional ethics, Mr Benedict. I have no option but to inform the authorities—'

At this, Fire shook her head. 'You can't . . . You've no idea what my mother . . .' She stopped then, stared down at her knees. 'At least, don't report them right away.'

'I will have to make the report within the next few days . . .'

Fire made a despairing sound and grasped my hand.

I thanked the specialist, assisted Fire from the consulting room and walked her slowly from the building. We caught a cab back to the gliding club.

'What am I going to do, Ben?' Fire asked.

She sat very still, as if paralysed, next to me.

'I can't go back home,' she said as we passed through the busy streets.

My mouth was suddenly dry. 'Don't worry, I don't intend to take you back.' I was aware that she was watching me.

'I can stay with you?' she asked.

I nodded. 'For as long as you like.'

We made the return flight in silence, each absorbed in our own thoughts. The archipelago passed beneath us, each knot of land identical to the last in everything but size. As Abe's island and then mine came into view, I was conscious of contrary and hypocritical emotions within me: I felt a numbed and constant ache at the loss of Abe, and at the same time a burgeoning joy that I had at last won Fire.

We ate on the patio overlooking the ocean. Later, we drank cheap brandy, watched the approach of the floating shield and talked. We talked of Earth and far-flung colony planets and places we would like to visit, but behind our conversation was the unspoken fact of what we had experienced today.

Fire piled a stack of magazines on her lap and leafed through them one by one. She came across a pamphlet advertising Abe's animal sanctuary. She looked up from it to the island across the sea.

'What about all the animals?' she murmured.

'The animals . . . ?'

'Out there, on the island. How will they live without Abe?' She looked at me. 'Bob, we must go over there and release them, OK? It's what Abe would have wanted. We can't let them stay there, imprisoned . . .' She shivered. 'That would be terrible . . .'

I put my arm around her shoulder and watched the shield usher in another night. The twilight deepened, moved through indigo to dark blue, then black. In the distance, the snow-capped mountains of Darkside glittered beneath a field of stars. On Abe's island, a dark silhouette against the lighter sea, the halogens in the domes winked on one by one, simulating the natural daylight of Brightside. I wondered how many times I had sat here on the patio, gazed out at the same scene and made the steadfast resolve to visit Abe.

We sat in silence and watched the pterosaurs make their way to Brightside.

Later, drunk on brandy, Fire took my hand and stared at me. Tears filled her eyes. 'Jade . . .' she whispered. 'My mother wiped Jade's accident from my mind.' She paused there and frowned. 'And Hannah Rodriguez. I can't remember anything about her! Why would Tamara not want me to remember her, Bob?'

'Hannah too?' I felt sick inside.

Fire nodded, too choked to speak. I drew her to me, found her lips, and the kiss was like a consummation, an affirmation of loyalty after all we had gone through together. She clung to me, more in desperation than affection.

We undressed each other slowly. She parted my shirt, traced the mess of scars on my chest with her fingertips. Her eyes looked into mine. 'Bob?'

'I was lucky,' I whispered.

That night, I dreamed of the accident. Again I was strapped into the command nexus, again I was powerless, through a combination of negligence and panic, to prevent the crash. The ship tumbled out of control towards the surface of Mars, and in the explosion that followed I heard the accusing screams of the hundred dying passengers.

I awoke suddenly and sat up in bed. I had gone through this so often in the past, alone: the hours of remorse, the surrender to the oblivion of frost . . . Now I felt Fire beside me, the line of her spine illuminated in the starlight, and the terror of the accident, and my guilt, became bearable.

Only then did I realize that she was crying. I lay down beside her and drew her warm body to mine. 'Fire . . . Fire,' I said, 'I miss him, too.'

It was some time before the tears stopped and she could bring herself to speak. Her head turned in the darkness and she looked at me.

'I'm crying for Jade . . .' she said.

7

BETRAYAL

That morning, as the floating shield moved gradually from the face of Beta Hydri and sunlight cascaded into the room, I lay on my back in a state of semi-sleep and thought of Fire, recalling the intimacies we had shared that night. I stared out through the dome and considered the year which had brought me to this point, and specifically the party at which I first met Fire. On reflection, the meeting had been the consequence of so many unlikely events – Abe's invitation, my decision to go, my chance encounter with Fire on the beach – that the more natural course of events would have been for us never to have met at all, and that thought was frightening.

Fire's place in the bed beside me was empty; only her scent remained, the impression of her head on the pillow. The evidence of her recent presence made the thought of her return a luxury. The fact that she was somewhere in the dome, in the bathroom or kitchen, until now used only by myself, seemed to bond us even further in a ritual of domesticity that I found both novel and reassuring.

I relaxed in the warming rays of the sun. For the first time in three days, I was not suffering the effects of withdrawal. I felt better than I had for a long time.

Activated by the timer, the music system played a soft, alien melody through the dome: Martian tablas, water-pipes and a female soprano singing in some colonial language made mysterious and significant by the fact that I could understand not a word. I was eager to know what Fire thought of the piece, one of my favourites.

I considered the many aspects of Fire unknown to me, like this one: the fact that she was an early riser. Which, when I thought about it, was understandable. For years her mother had insisted that she retire early, for her health. It would be a while before she learnt to overcome the many habits of her conditioning.

It had occurred to me again, while lying awake in the early hours with Fire in my arms, that if Steiner's adviser connected me with Abe, then I was in danger. It had seemed melodramatic then to think in these terms: but the fact was that Abe was dead, murdered by Weller because he knew too much. I resolved now to take Fire to one of the smaller island-towns beyond Main, to lie low for a time, even to begin a new life . . .

I rose and left the lounge. Fire was not in the bathroom, so I showered and made my way to the kitchen. While the percolator brewed the coffee, I stepped out into the small garden. I imagined I might find Fire there, stretched out in the sun. I returned inside, collected a coffee, and went through into the lounge. She was not there either and, though the dome had about it a quiet and stillness that suggested I was its only occupant, I was not unduly worried. I strode out on to the patio and surveyed the path down to the bay.

'Fire . . . ?' I heard the note of concern in my voice and censored myself. I was suddenly tortured by the notion that she had left me, but this was so outrageous that it only heightened my anticipation of the moment she would show herself: she was obviously playing a game. The sensation of imminence burned within my chest like joy or excitement.

'Fire . . . I know you're hiding.' I rushed inside, through the lounge, to the other rooms I had not yet checked. On entering each one I expected to find her there, cowering in delight. But she was in none of the upper rooms of the dome, and the hatch to the basement was locked.

In panic now, torn between the desire to delude myself further with thoughts that I would soon find her, and the unimaginable possibility that for some reason she had indeed left the island, I returned to the patio and made my way down the winding path. There was still a large part of the island I had not yet searched. Fire might have taken it into her head to go for a morning walk.

Half-way down the path, between the dome and the cove, I came to a stop. I made out two small dark shapes on the ocean, approaching the island. As I watched, the launches parted company; one continued towards the cove, the other veered off around the island. The first launch beached itself and half a dozen guards in black uniforms – familiar from Trevellion's island – alighted and surveyed the terrain.

I turned and hurried back to the dome; the invasion of Trevellion's guards, far from causing me concern, eased my apprehension. Clearly, Fire had either foreseen the event, or had actually spotted the approach of the craft, and in panic had gone to earth. It occurred to me that she might have had time to leave some note or message detailing her plans. I chose to ignore the fact that she might just as easily have woken me and told me of the danger: I managed to convince myself that she did not want to worry me at the time. I searched the lounge, but there was no sign of a note.

At least, now, I had an explanation for her disappearance.

I returned to the patio. The guards were jogging up the path. I experienced a sudden and intense burst of fury: they were responsible for Fire's flight, and anyway had no right to trespass on my domain. I imagined Tamara Trevellion, back on her island, conducting the operation like a spider at the centre of her web of intrigue.

I calmed myself as the guards turned the last bend and climbed towards the patio. I would play the innocent party, deny all knowledge of Fire's present whereabouts, claim that I was alone and had been for hours. In other words, I would be telling the truth. My only worry was that the second group of guards, swarming over the island from the rear, would find Fire before I convinced this party that she had departed during the night.

They halted before me, led by the same squat thug who had turned me back from Trevellion's island yesterday morning.

'Where is she, Benedict?'

I feigned surprise. 'Fire? She left last night. She took the evening ferry to Main.' As soon as I said this, I knew I had made a mistake. The ferry made two trips a day to Main, stopping off at the islands of the archipelago when requested. All the guard had to do was contact the ferry company and check the passenger manifesto.

He nodded to his men, who brushed past me and entered the lounge. While the leader regarded me with the same negligent contempt he had exhibited yesterday, I could hear the other guards going through the dome room by room.

He strolled over to the drinks' dispenser, dialled himself a beer, then moved to the edge of the patio and lodged a boot on the low wall. He spoke briefly into his handset, then chugged the beer while awaiting a reply. It occurred to me that his studious disregard of my presence was designed to unsettle me.

His handset bleeped and the small face on his metacarpal screen spoke. The exchange lasted barely five seconds. I swallowed, aware that my lie had been found out. The guard drained the carton, tossed it into the shrubbery beyond the patio and returned to where I was standing.

'You're lying, Benedict. She wasn't on the ferry last night.' He watched me, waiting.

I shrugged. 'I didn't see her set off. She left me in the dome. I presumed she took the ferry.' We had reached an impasse. I was amazed that I had remained so calm.

'We'll find her, Benedict, sooner or later. She can only run so far.'

He looked up past the apex of the dome, smiled to himself. Over the highest peak on the island, half a kilometre away, a guard hung from a jet-pack in the air. As I watched, he methodically played a heat-seeking implement, like a shoulder camera, across the length and breadth of the island. The sight had the effect of damping my spirits; my hope that Fire was hiding out somewhere and might go undetected seemed in vain.

The guard was watching me with something like pity in his eyes. He shook his head. 'I don't know why you do it, Benedict. Won't you ever learn?' Did I detect genuine concern in his tone?

I tried to stare him out. 'Do what?'

He laughed. 'Don't play the fool, Benedict. You know what I'm talking about. Look, there's a whole island full of women up at Main. Why don't you chase them?'

'They aren't Fire,' I said, defiant.

'Too right, man.' He helped himself to another beer, turned and gestured with the carton. 'First Steiner and Jade, then you with Fire. What is it with you good Samaritans?' He hesitated. 'Benedict, take my advice. Leave Fire well alone. She's forbidden fruit. She belongs to Tamara Trevellion, and you shouldn't play with what belongs to Trevellion.'

'You make her sound like property,' I said.

He laughed. 'And she isn't?' He stared at me. 'Benedict, forget you ever saw Fire. Don't get on the wrong side of Trevellion. She can be one mean bitch if you cross her.'

'You sound as if you despise the woman.'

He finished his beer, watched the empty carton sail over the edge of the patio, considering. 'In my line of work, Benedict, personal feelings don't enter into the matter. Trevellion's my employer. I follow her orders.'

'And you have no qualms about taking Fire back to the life she leads on Trevellion's island?'

'Could be worse. She has it easy, compared to some.'

'She's old enough to lead her own life, where and how she wants.'

'She's ill, Benedict,' he said, repeating the old lie. 'She needs the treatment only Trevellion's surgeon can give.'

I was on the verge of putting him right, but stopped myself. I remained silent, let him think he'd won the argument.

A dozen guards came around the dome and made their reports. I was at once relieved that they had failed to find Fire, and concerned as to her whereabouts. They were joined by the guards who had searched the dome, and they too had found nothing. The leader nodded, dismissed them; they retreated down the path to the cove.

The head guard once again consulted his handset. This time I made out the unmistakable face of Tamara Trevellion. The guard said, 'Yes, yes of course.' He seemed chastened.

He switched off his handset and regarded me.

'That was Trevellion. She wants me to bring you in for questioning. You know what that means? They say that her surgeon doesn't restrict himself only to the healing practices . . .'

My mouth went dry. I think I even smiled. 'You can't do that. Trevellion has no authority—'

The guard grinned. 'You're shit scared, Benedict.'

I was, but I was damned if I was going to admit it. 'I happen to be a friend of Inspector Foulds—' I began.

The guard laughed. ' "I happen to be a friend of Inspector Foulds," ' he mimicked.

I tried to sound confident. 'You can't take me . . .'

'If you tell me where Fire is, we'll do a deal. I won't take you in. How does that sound?'

'As I said before, I don't know where she is.'

The guard smiled to himself. 'It sounds to me that if you did know, then you'd give her away. Where's your loyalty, Benedict?'

'I wouldn't tell you even if I did know,' I said. 'She left sometime last night.' I realized that I was sweating – not only at the prospect of being taken in, but at the thought that I *really* did not know where Fire was, or why she had left. What one hour ago had been an idyll, was now a hell.

'You know something, Benedict? I'm tempted to believe you.'

'It's the truth . . .'

He nodded. 'I'll tell you what, I won't take you in. We'll go and search Main Island. Then, if we still haven't found her, we'll come back for you.'

'You're bluffing,' I managed. 'Even Trevellion wouldn't do that.'

'No?' He seemed amused. 'Well, we'll see about that.'

He took one last comprehensive look around the patio in case he'd missed some vital clue, then turned and walked quickly down the path to the bay. I watched him go, my relief increasing with his every step away from the dome. He joined his men in the first launch. The vehicle rose, turned on its axis and headed out to sea. The second launch appeared and followed the first. I watched them until they were obscured by the projecting headland, then slumped into the foam-form. My relief was short-lived: the image of Fire, lost and in need of help, came to me. I hurried into the lounge, part of me still crazily convinced, despite all logic, that she was hiding somewhere in the dome. I called her name, told her that the guards had gone and she could come out now.

The lounge was in a state of disarray. Furniture had been moved, shelves pulled from the walls – as if Fire could have been hiding behind them! – in a vindictive display of force. I assumed every room in the dome was like this one, and I experienced a burning sense of injustice. My only consolation was that they had not found what they had come for.

I paused by the wall unit on which I kept the vid-discs; it too had been pulled out. I stared at the niche in the wall behind it. Last night, as a precaution I hated myself for taking, I had removed the half-shell of frost from the coffee table and concealed it behind the unit. I had made sure that Fire was elsewhere before doing this – at least, I *thought* I had – but either she had seen me, or had searched the dome in desperation until finding my hiding place: the niche was empty. The half-shell was missing.

I hurried from the lounge, too shocked to consider the implications of what Fire had done. It was imperative now that I locate her. I tried to clear my mind and concentrate on where she might have gone. If the guards were correct in their assumption that she was no longer on the island, then she must have left by one of the two means available – by launch or by glider. As she had no experience piloting a glider, that left the launch. I ran from the patio and down the path. I came to the cove and ran along the jetty. Sure enough, the launch was missing. I just stood and stared at the vacant berth, and as I did so I recalled the brochure Fire had leafed through last night – and her request to go to Abe's island today. If she had guessed that her mother would send out the guards, then the island would provide the perfect hiding place in which to use the drug.

I sprinted to the boathouse where I stored the glider, hauled it out and set about preparing it for flight. Five minutes later I strapped myself into the harness, hit the starter and soared into the air above the bay. I turned inland, cut across the incline and the pathway so as to put the bulk of the island between myself and the direction the guards had taken, then accelerated out across the open ocean, wave-hopping.

Abe's island was only a kilometre away from mine, but the journey seemed to take an age. As I went, I tried to convince myself that one of the guards had stolen the frost, but try as I might I could recall no one trying to conceal something as bulky as the half-shell on leaving the lounge.

The plain fact was that Fire had taken the frost, and I could understand her need to know whether the death of her sister had been an accident, or suicide. She had begged me to let her have the drug, but I had refused – and she had gone behind my back and stolen it. But I still felt betrayed. As I approached Abe's island, I resolved to ask Fire one question, one very simple question: I wanted to know if I meant anything at all to her, or if her show of affection over the period we had known each other had been nothing more than a ploy.

I came down gently on the path leading to Abe's villa, then concealed the glider among the shrubbery. Down below, in the bay, I could see my launch, moored to the jetty. As I began the climb to the villa, I was conscious of my increased pulse. I considered the times I had made this journey in the past, to share a beer and a quiet chat with Abe, and how very different the circumstances were now.

Now that the time had arrived to confront Fire, I approached the verandah with apprehension, the words I had arranged to say a jumble in my head. She was not on the verandah. I stepped through the open sliding doors to the lounge, and was immediately assailed by the tantalizing scent, pungent and bitter, of burnt frost. I coughed, wafted away the fumes which hung in the air. I heard the sound of something move, and saw a blurred shape head for the door – Abe's pet pterosaur.

In the event, I did not have the opportunity to question Fire. She was sprawled on the chesterfield, her arms and legs spread in a posture of submission to the drug. The half-shell lay on the floor where she'd dropped it. I knelt beside Fire and took her hand. Her pulse was slow, her breathing shallow. New to frost, she had misused it, inhaled too much. This was not dangerous in itself, but it did mean that the quality of the recalled event – the death of her sister, presumably – would be enhanced, prolonged. There was nothing I could do but be with her when she came to her senses.

I opened an inside door and the rear exit to create a draught and clear the air, then returned to her side. So far, my only thought had been to find Fire and question her – I had looked no further. What mattered now was to get Fire as far away as possible from her mother's henchmen. We had the perfect means of escape – the glider – and could depart just as soon as Fire regained consciousness. We would then proceed, as planned, to an island beyond Main.

A shadow fell across the room. I turned. A figure stood in the doorway. I could not make out his face against the bright light outside, but the cut of the uniform was familiar. He advanced, and I could see that his side-arm was drawn and directed at me.

It speaks volumes for human fortitude, or sheer stupidity, that even in this situation I was thinking desperately of a way that Fire and I might escape the guard, make it to the glider and leave the island without being followed . . . Then more guards tumbled into the room, and it was with real shock that I realized we were going nowhere, that they would overcome me and return Fire to her mother, no matter what I did.

Even so, I dived at the leading guard with the vague notion of disarming him and blasting our way free. I was burning on raw anger, without a thought for practicalities. By comparison to the guard in the area of physical combat, I was an amateur; he knew what he was doing and he handled me with contemptuous efficiency. I failed to see him move, but I felt what might have been a boot planted firmly in my solar plexus, followed by a fist in my face, and I was flat on my back on the floor. I gasped for breath, nauseous, and the guards simply ignored me. They surrounded Fire, thumbed open her eyelids and checked her pulse. This done, one of their number unceremoniously lifted her and slung her over his shoulder, so that her long golden hair hung parallel to her tanned arms. They filed from the room without so much as a backward glance, left me cursing them in silence and holding back my tears. I tried to console myself with the thought that they would have searched Abe's island sooner or later, and that my leading them here had only brought forward the inevitable.

I was a long time on the floor, regaining my breath. I staggered to my feet and stumbled out on to the verandah. There was no sign of the launches on the sea. I dialled myself a cold drink from the dispenser and drank it as if I were dying of thirst. As the minutes passed, and the sense of injustice at what had happened began to abate, I came to see Fire's abduction as only an early move in the game of intrigue between Trevellion and myself – not the ultimate act of triumph on her part. Trevellion might have succeeded in recapturing her daughter for the time being, but the move was wholly against Fire's will, and I did not intend to sit back and admit defeat. Quite how I should proceed, though, was another question.

I looked around me at the island and thought of Abe. I had only ever been here in his presence before, and his absence now gave the villa and the island a terrible atmosphere of desolation, an air of redundancy. Everything I looked at, be it the drinks' dispenser on the verandah, the low wall where he had often paused to gaze out to sea, reminded me of him. I expected to see Abe emerge from the lounge at any second.

I recalled Fire's strange, if oddly appropriate, reaction last night, when she had insisted that the animals should be set free. I stepped from the veranda and took the path towards the cages and domes which held the various specimens of Meridian wildlife. These animals could survive in their enclosures indefinitely – they were fed and watered by a complex computerized system which Abe had designed himself – but their continued captivity, when Abe was no longer around to continue his work, seemed a crime. One by one I opened the cages and domes, then stood back as the animals inside either took full advantage and scampered to freedom, or cowered suspiciously in the security of their artificial habitats, regarding me dubiously. Those animals which took their liberty, and disappeared into the surrounding vegetation, filled me with a strange sense of joy.

One hour later all the cages and domes were open, and most of them were empty; from the dense green shrubbery of the island arose a chorus of birdsong, howls and grunts as if in lament at Abe's passing. My clothes wet with sweat, I made my way back up to the villa and helped myself to another beer.

I was considering what to do next when Abe's pterosaur flapped from an overhanging tree and landed on the verandah. It stropped its bill against my leg and squawked in a manner I interpreted as forlorn. We stared at each other for a long time, communicating some notion of our incommunicable tragedy. Then, on impulse, I stood and gathered up the bird and, despite its protests, ran to the edge of the verandah and pitched it into the air. It flapped frantically, plummeted in a flurry of beating wings and desperately pedalling legs, then gained purchase on the air and soared majestically, neck outthrust in a gesture of indignation. It swooped out to sea, sending a thrill down my spine at the fact of its freedom – then turned back and came to rest on a headland perhaps five hundred metres distant. Defiantly, it flapped its wings once or twice, then folded them away with an air of finality. I cursed the bird and pitched my empty beer carton feebly in its direction. As I watched, the pterosaur waved its wings in agitation and dived into the cover of a nearby bush – not put out at my projectile, but at the arrival on the scene of a much bigger bird.

The helicab swung into sight over the headland, hovered and came to rest amid a swirling sandstorm on the beach at the foot of the path. At this distance, I could not make out the lettering on the flank of the bulbous fuselage, but the white logo on the blue field was unmistakable: the three scimitars, point to point to point, of the Telemass Organization. The rotors slowed, drooped to resemble palm leaves. Someone climbed from the passenger's seat, removed his helmet and flung it back into the cab. He shielded his eyes, gazed up the hillside, then trudged across the beach and up the path. As he approached, I saw that he was small, dark-haired, and bearded: Steiner's technical adviser, Weller.

When it became obvious that he was making his way to the villa, I slipped from the verandah and concealed myself in the surrounding jungle. Weller paused a matter of metres from me, a laser pistol in his hand, and looked around. For a terrible second I thought that he must have seen me from the beach – then, to my relief, he stepped through the open doors into the villa. For the next thirty minutes I heard the constant sizzle of laser fire, and the popping and burning of targeted objects. At one point the island shook with the impact of an explosion, followed by the greedy crackle of flames. I curled in a ball and wrapped my arms about my head.

When the firing stopped, I cautiously peered through the foliage. Weller emerged on the verandah, and through the door to the lounge I could see the burnt and twisted remains of Abe's belongings. A rear room was burning fiercely, and soon the villa was one raging inferno. The heat of its incineration hit me in a wave, rendering me breathless. It was all I could do not to gag on the billowing smoke and give myself away.

Weller holstered his pistol and jumped from the verandah. I watched him retrace his steps down the path and across the beach, leaving a trail of symmetrical prints in the sand alongside those he had made on his way from the 'cab. He replaced his helmet, gazed back at the pyre of Abe's villa, and climbed back into the helicab. It rose, tipped nose-down and clattered away from the beach. The downdraught from its rotors hit the sand and churned it for a radius of fifty metres, obliterating totally all sign of Weller's footprints.

I stared at the flattened swath of sand with sudden understanding . . .

I waited until the helicab was a tiny speck in the distance, heading for Main, then ran down the path to where Fire had moored my launch. I jumped aboard, gunned the engine and steered from the bay towards my island. By the time I beached the launch and sprinted up to my dome, I was sick with apprehension.

I had to calm myself as I sat before the screen. I imagined the dishevelled sight I would present to Doug, then dismissed it as irrelevant. What mattered was what I had to tell him.

I got through to his office.

A secretary answered and told me that Doug had left thirty minutes ago.

'Could you put me through to him?'

'I'm afraid not. I could let you speak to his deputy—'

'I need to see the Inspector. Did he tell you where he was going?'

'One minute . . .' The secretary consulted another screen. 'He's attending an event on Trevellion's island, but he left instructions that he wasn't to be—'

I cut the connection, sat staring at the blank screen. In the confusion of the past day, I had quite forgotten about Trevellion's forthcoming live event; to which, I recalled, she had invited me. I had the urge to make my way there immediately, create a scene and demand the return of Fire . . . Then I had second thoughts. If I arrived exhibiting belligerence, Trevellion would have no qualms about having her henchmen forcibly eject me. However, if I turned up suitably attired and composed, as if outwardly accepting my defeat, then perhaps she might honour her invitation.

Thirty minutes later I made my way for the last time to Trevellion's island.

THE ULTIMATE EVENT

Darkness was descending by the time I reached the island. Already the party was under way. A band played loud, throbbing music, the noise meeting me as I drifted into the marina. On the summit of the island the dome was aglow, and beside it the lawn was illuminated like a sporting venue. I made the launch fast to the quayside and stepped out, recalling that, just a few days earlier, Abe Cunningham had accompanied me to the last event. There were fewer boats in the marina now, and consequently not as many guests waiting at the foot of the escalator which zig-zagged up the hillside. The two couples before me introduced themselves to the armed guard. They were allowed through with polite smiles and nods of courtesy. When it was my turn to pass muster, the guard blocked my way.

'Benedict,' I said. 'Trevellion invited me.'

The guard turned and spoke into his handset.

There might not have been as many guests present tonight, but there was a disproportionate number of guards stationed around the marina, and at strategic positions up the switchback escalator. As far as I could make out, none of these individuals were among the band of thugs which had raided first my island, and then Abe's, earlier in the day. I wondered if Trevellion had increased the numbers of her private army for tonight and, if so, why.

Still speaking into his handset, the guard turned to me and looked me up and down. He gestured curtly for me to pass. I tried to ignore him as I did so, but it was more difficult to ignore the stares of the dozen other guards on the way up. They made it clear that I was, despite my invitation, *persona non grata* here tonight. I was relieved that I had forgone earlier rash plans to take the island by storm and rescue Fire single-handed.

A servant – I noticed others stationed at the entrances to various passages – ushered me through the dome to the illuminated lawn. Again, like last time, my name was announced, along with my ex-profession. Again it caused the same lack of interest. A crowd of Altered, Augmenteds, and normals chatted animatedly on the lawn. I recognized Leo Realisto and Trixi the bush-baby, and hurried past before they saw me. Euphor-fumes fulminated from burners set on pedestals, the columns of smoke showing blue, green, and red in the light from the floating lanterns. I resolved not to get too near the things. I wanted to be sober when I confronted Trevellion.

Fire was nowhere to be seen among the gathered guests, not that I'd expected her to be on show so soon after her abduction. Nor was Tamara Trevellion, though if she followed form she would make her grand entry later in the evening. I plucked a drink from a passing tray and surveyed the crowd for Doug Foulds, without success. There was much hilarity in the air, which was to be expected with the liberal placement of the euphor-fumes, but underlying the gaiety was a quite definite sense of anticipation. In the night sky above the adjacent greensward, I made out a large rectangular object, for all the world like an airborne stage.

I bumped into an acquaintance – someone whose launch I had once repaired – and we chatted for a while. I felt uncomfortable, and the fact that I'd found someone to talk to hardly helped matters. I was frustrated at being so close to Fire, and yet so powerless even to meet her, let alone take her away from here. I had to maintain a show of polite interest now that I was here, an act of bonhomie I did not feel, while at the same time wondering if, at the end of the night, I would be reunited with Fire – always supposing, that was, that Fire wanted to be reunited.

I moved on, finding that if I kept on walking I did not feel so conspicuous. I kept this up for perhaps fifteen minutes, then sat side-saddle on the long balustrade in the cover of a sculpture, affecting a pose of solitary interest in the view of the night-time sea. From this position, I could make out the upper curve of Fire's dome. It was illuminated from inside, suggesting that someone was in the room. I plotted a course through the shrubbery, and at the same time checked the positions of the guards around the lawn. By now, Fire would have regained consciousness after her trip, and if only I could make it to her dome undetected . . .

I was about to move towards the Meridian cacti, the first place of concealment *en route* to her dome, when the floating speaker announced the arrival of Director Wolfe Steiner and Guy Weller, his technical adviser.

I felt a curious emptiness as Director Steiner stepped from the dome, followed by the short beaded man I had seen that afternoon. I should perhaps have experienced anger and outrage at that moment, as heads turned and a polite patter of applause rippled among the gathering, but, although I was just a stone's throw from Abe Cunningham's killer, I was aware only of a negation of feeling within me. I think I realized even then that Weller and Steiner were no more than pawns moved in some game of Expansionist power-politics to eliminate pieces which had strayed quite by accident into the path of progress – though what progress, to what end, I did not know. I recalled someone, I think it was Doug, telling me that Steiner was a puppet at the beck and call of his superiors on Earth, and I think that I even began, without quite knowing why, to sympathize with the Augmented Director. He stood at the top of the steps, surveying the gathering with his rather imperious, upright demeanour. He descended into the crowd and circulated, closely followed by his adviser.

I felt suddenly removed from the reality of the party, alienated. I recalled the many incidents of the past few days, and knew that my experience of these events was what put me on the outside of this gathering, that it had little to do with the fact of my physical isolation. I pitied the guests, the insular, comfortable coterie of artists and agents and hangers-on – I pitied their ignorance of the fact that something significant was occurring beneath the surface of their everyday lives. Or perhaps my pity was nothing more than a defence mechanism; perhaps I wished that I too was just as ignorant.

My attention was caught by activity across the lawn. A spotlight picked out the arched exit of the dome, and the babble of the crowd modulated to a low murmur of expectation. Heads turned, and those guests without a view moved so that they might witness Trevellion's entry. From my position on the balustrade, I could see over the crowd to the marble steps bathed in silver light. As I watched, Trevellion stepped into the circle of illumination, her surgeon in close attendance. She paused before a floating microphone, inclining her head in minimal acknowledgement of the applause. She wore a golden shawl wrapped about her body and draped over one shoulder, and a matching tiara. It was perhaps some measure of how important she considered this particular event that she had bothered to dress for it.

Her cold, precise voice cut through and silenced the murmurs from the crowd. 'Ladies and gentlemen ... It is, as ever, an honour to have you here ...' As she spoke, I considered taking the opportunity, while the attention of the crowd was on Trevellion, to move off and attempt to find Fire. But something about Trevellion's tone, and later the content of the speech, kept me listening. She seemed, as I listened to the mundane preamble of pleasantries, a little more animated than usual, even excited. Compared with her usual icy monotone, her voice was imbued with emotion. At the same time it struck me that her speech had something of the farewell address about it. 'Many of you here tonight have been my loyal friends and colleagues for the many years I have made my home on Meridian. I came here as an unknown artist, and for years have worked to change that. Only of late have I been able to say with any confidence that I have come close to fulfilling my potential. Tonight, I believe, I have created a work which will stand for ever as a statement on transplanetary colonialism – a work which will, I hope, resonate in retrospect with cosmic truths. I thank you for your support and friendship over the years.' She gave a small bow, and a burst of applause sounded around the lawn. She held up an arm, connected to her body by a thin, webbed veil. At first I took the gesture to be one of valediction; then, as the crowd silenced itself, I knew that Trevellion had not yet finished her speech.

'A few words, if I may, about tonight's event.' For perhaps five minutes she lost me with arcane, and probably meaningless, references to metaphor, symbolism, the place of live events in the pantheon of modern arts, and *performance*. She stressed the word, and went on to say that what we were about to witness was a construction of effect produced by techniques of artistry unknown to Meridian. By this time, the crowd was in a foam of delight at the prospect of the treat. I, for my part, saw Trevellion only as a charlatan, a pretender in the field of artistic endeavour whose soul was as corrupt as she fancied her talent to be great. She held aloft a webbed palm to dampen the chorus of speculation. 'The event will commence in one hour.' She stepped from the marble staircase and was immediately surrounded by Trixi, Realisto, and the rest of her fan club.

While all the attention was focused on Trevellion's progress through the throng of her admirers, I ensured that the guards stationed around the garden were looking elsewhere. Then I casually left the balustrade and stepped behind the sheltering cacti, paused and considered my next move.

I judged that more than two hundred metres separated my present position from Fire's dome. Most of that distance was concealed from the lawn and the guards by an ornamental hedge and behind it a mass of tropical bushes – but I had no idea if any guards were stationed among the shrubbery, or if the area was under surveillance by remote-control cameras.

I hurried on to the next point of cover, and from there passed deeper into the surrounding vegetation. Soon I lost sight of the guests on the lawn; even the music seemed distant, muffled by the intervening foliage. As I hurried through the darkened undergrowth, I came across neither guards or security cameras. I ran doubled-up towards the dome, showing as lighted sparks and slivers between leaf and branch.

I came to the edge of the garden and dropped into the cover of a bush. Miraculously, it seemed that the dome was unguarded. In the golden glow of light that spilled from the dome itself, I made out no threatening, black-uniformed figures. All was still, quiet. The party proceeding on the far side of the main dome might have been a million miles away.

My pulse increased as I transferred my attention from the garden to the dome. I took a breath as I saw Fire inside, seated cross-legged on the circular bed, with her elbows on her knees and her head in her hands. She wore a white gown, with her long blonde hair braided and coiled about her head. It seemed to me that she had never looked more beautiful.

So far my passage here had been easy, but I knew that that could not last. In the back of my mind I was aware that I'd had it *too* easy

– and the pessimist in me was expecting the worst. I made sure one last time that the way was clear, then dashed across the crescent lawn to the clear wall of the dome.

From this angle, Fire could not see me. I moved carefully around the perimeter of the dome towards the hatch, then stopped. Now I was in her line of sight – or would have been had she held her head upright. She was regarding the bowl of her crossed legs in an attitude of sadness or loss and my presence, mere metres from her, went unnoticed. I rapped on the wall of the dome, expecting an immediate, delighted response. Instead, she looked up slowly and regarded me with the same large, emerald eyes of old, though dulled now, as if drugged. Her expression – or, rather, her distinct lack of expression – did not alter. She stared at me with neutral incomprehension, as if she had never seen me before in her life.

'Fire!' I called. I grabbed the handle and tried to open the hatch, but it resisted my pressure.

As if in response to my cry, a flicker of something briefly animated her eyes: troubled confusion, as if she was aware that she *should* know me, but nevertheless did not. Her lips moved to form a moue of pained contemplation. A cold weight of dread settled in my chest. 'Fire!' I called again, heedless of the attention I might attract. I gestured for her to come to me, to open the hatch.

With the graceful movements of a narcoleptic ballerina, she unfolded herself from the sitting position and stepped across the room, the white gown flowing in her wake. Mystification clouded her eyes, even entered her expression: she was frowning, as if questioning herself as to whether what she was doing was right. I found her doubt even more painful than her earlier, blank expression.

'What have they done to you, Fire?'

I spread a hand on the glass dividing us, and, like a mirror image delayed by seconds, she matched the gesture with her own small hand. 'Fire . . . open the hatch.' I indicated the catch mechanism on the inner rim of the arched exit. Her hand dropped to the catch, her fingers gripped it and she grimaced with effort as she attempted to force it down. As she tried repeatedly and failed, her gaze looked through the glass, at me, and it seemed that some light of recognition stirred within her – recognition at once reassuring and terrible: she might have begun to realize who I was, but she was also coming to some understanding that she was imprisoned against her will.

When it became obvious to her that the hatch was locked, her hand fell to her side in helplessness.

'Never mind. Can you hear me?'

She nodded.

It was some time before I could bring myself to ask, 'Fire, can you remember me?'

A delay. Uncertainty. Then, almost grudgingly, another, smaller nod.

I released a pent-up breath, confident that her confusion was the result of a drug administered to keep her under sedation, and not an amnesiac. 'Good . . . Great.' I paused there, uncertain how to continue. Then, 'Can you do as I tell you, Fire? Do you understand?'

She frowned, nodded almost imperceptibly.

I went on, 'Leave your room without anyone seeing you – can you do that? Come round the main dome to this garden. I'll meet you here. Then we'll take the tunnel.'

She was nodding, as if in eagerness.

'Go on, then.'

After a delay of seconds she turned and walked towards the door which connected her room to the main dome. I watched her go, my heart racing. I had a vague plan in mind: I would take her down to the beach, return to my launch and pick her up. Then we would leave for a distant island and lie low while Trevellion's men scoured the planet.

She had hardly passed from sight before she returned, her movements just as lacklustre. I felt a surge of despair at her failure to follow the simple command – then I saw the guard, tall and intimidating, stationed in the doorway behind her. He was staring directly at me and, before my despair at Fire's failure to escape could turn to rage, a hand closed on my upper arm, in a gesture almost gentle.

'Benedict . . .' The tone seemed sincerely pained. I turned to see the guard who, just that afternoon, had beaten me senseless.

Tamara Trevellion strode around the curve of the dome, her spined crest bristling with anger. She halted and regarded me with those flat, grey and vacant eyes. 'Benedict,' she said. 'I might have known.'

The golden wrap she wore coiled about her body and flung over one shoulder, far from conferring her with humanity, had the very opposite effect: it served only to emphasize the fact of her alien appearance. I found it hard to believe that a human mind, with the usual complement of emotions we take for granted in a fellow citizen, functioned between the flattened, elongated ridges of her skull.

Fire remained standing in the middle of her room, staring at nothing.

I was aware of the guard's grip on my arm, restraining me from doing anything I might later regret. I worked to keep my voice under control. 'Why the hell are you keeping her imprisoned?'

The gills at her throat opened, showing raw, red vents, in a gesture I thought might indicate impatience. She waved. 'Return him to the party, Tanner.'

The guard moved to comply.

'I know what you did to her,' I began.

This had an immediate effect. In the process of turning, she stopped. Her head, itself like an individual fish, turned to regard me independent of her body. Her expression gave nothing away, but her silence spoke volumes.

She dismissed Tanner. The scales of her mailed cheeks glittered like sequins in the light from the dome.

'Perhaps, Mr Benedict, you might like to explain exactly what you mean by that?'

I thought quickly. I decided to keep to myself the fact that I knew there was nothing wrong with Fire.

Instead I said, 'You've used the implant to drug her . . .'

She considered me. 'Benedict, your concern for Fire is shared by me, which is why she had to be treated, for her own good.'

I stared at the fish-woman. 'Just as Jade had to be *treated* – for her own good? You implanted her too, didn't you?'

She held her ground. 'Jade was ill, Benedict. She had a similar condition to Fire's, which had to be monitored. We had to equip her with an implant.'

I refrained from calling her a liar. 'And it was just coincidence that these implants could be used to administer drugs, too?' I shook my head. 'You wanted to control your daughters' lives, to make them totally subservient, because of some inferiority of your own. No doubt that's why Jade killed herself – she'd had enough of your mental cruelty.'

Her gills flapped open, shunting air.

I went on, 'And that's not the only death you know about, is it? You know why Rodriguez and Abe were killed—'

'Abraham?' She seemed genuinely shocked. 'Abraham Cunningham? I had no idea . . .'

'They were killed by Weller, Steiner's adviser. They knew too much about something.' I paused. 'Why did you wipe Fire's memory of Jade and Hannah Rodriguez?' I asked.

'How did you—' she began, then stopped herself.

'So you don't deny it?' I said. I stared at her. 'What the hell's going on, Trevellion?'

'Benedict . . .' I detected a harsh, threatening note in her voice.

'You're in this as deep as Steiner and Weller,' I said. 'Just wait till Doug Foulds finds out—'

Trevellion flung back her head and made a sound like laughter. 'As if Foulds could do anything!'

'We'll see,' I said, making to go.

She stopped me with her next words. 'Do you want to see Fire again after tonight, Benedict?'

I stared at her. 'What do you mean?'

'Just don't do anything to spoil tonight's event, and you might see Fire again. If you go around shouting murder . . .'

I looked through the dome at Fire. She was staring out from her crystal cage, a figure of tragedy, regarding me with unseeing eyes.

Quite suddenly I could no longer bear Trevellion's company. She seemed to exude, along with her odour of the sea, an aura of malign intent. I made a strangled sound of inarticulate disgust, hurried around the main dome and rejoined the party.

I snatched a drink from a floating tray and knocked it back in a fit of anger. I went over what I had said to Trevellion, and could not help feeling that I had let her off lightly. I wanted to confront her again, to be more forceful, perhaps even threaten her with physical violence.

I was taking a second drink when across the lawn I saw the stocky figure of Doug Foulds. He was standing next to a euphor-fume pedestal, glass in hand, laughing at something someone had told him. He appeared to be enjoying himself and, with two murders unsolved and investigations to be made, this infuriated me. I was checking to make sure that Trevellion was nowhere in sight when Doug turned and saw me. He seemed to sober instantly. He hurried across the lawn; I was conscious of the guards, hoped that my meeting with him would not get back to Trevellion. I had no doubt that if she wanted to keep Fire away from me in future she would have little difficulty in doing so.

Doug cleared his throat. 'Ah . . . Bob.'

I stared at him. 'Didn't you get my message yesterday to call me back?'

He looked uncomfortable, glanced around the gathering as if afraid we might be overheard. He took my arm and steered me to the perimeter of the garden and behind a squat steel sculpture, effectively shielding us from prying eyes. The privacy suited me fine, but I wondered why he thought it necessary.

'I know about Abe,' he said.

'You do?'

'That's what you called about yesterday, wasn't it? His body was discovered last night, and we traced your call from the hotel that afternoon.'

'Before you start suspecting me,' I said, 'I know who killed both Abe and the Rodriguez woman.'

'Go on.'

'I know who did it – all I need to know now is the motive. *Why* he killed Abe and Rodriguez. I'll leave that to you, though. I've had quite enough.' I stared at him. 'I suppose you want to know who *he* is?'

He looked me straight in the eye. 'I already know who killed Abe and Hannah,' he said.

Confusion, a feeling I was becoming well acquainted with of late, swamped me. 'You do? Then why the hell haven't you done something about it?' I gestured across the lawn to where Weller was in conversation with Steiner.

Doug glanced away, nervous. 'I've been promoted,' he said, in barely a whisper.

I shook my head, attempting to determine the logic of his words.

143

'Promoted? How the hell can you be promoted? You hold the top police job on the planet!'

'I'm being transferred. I leave Meridian for Earth tomorrow.'

'Congratulations,' I snapped. 'But that still doesn't explain why you haven't arrested Weller.' I stopped, then went on, 'The authorities on Earth have something to do with this, haven't they?'

'Look, Bob – I hate all this as much as you do. Abe was a friend of mine too. Yesterday I made some inquiries, found that Weller was seen entering the Meridian Star on the night of Abe's death. I took him in for questioning, but an hour later the Governor called and ordered me to release him. A short time later I was told I'd been promoted and would be leaving for Earth on the next vector out. Hell, Bob . . . I feel part of the whole corrupt set-up. But what can I do?'

'What's going on, Doug?' I murmured.

He shook his head. 'I honestly don't know.'

I made a hopeless gesture of defeat. 'Christ, can't you . . . I don't know – isn't there someone we can contact—?'

'Wake up, Bob,' Doug said, not unkindly. 'Who? Who the hell can we tell? I'd like to avenge Abe's death, but I don't want to die a martyr.' He looked at me with compassion. 'We're pawns, Bob. You and me, Abe, everyone else. Even Steiner. There's nothing we can do. We don't even understand the rules of the game . . . Take my advice. Go back to your island, forget what happened.'

His complacency detonated an explosion of anger deep inside me. 'Forget? Abe was a damn good friend, Doug – and you say forget?'

At that moment, the band stopped playing. For a second the murmurous conversation of the guests filled the silence, then this too ceased. All eyes turned to the dome, and Tamara Trevellion made her second triumphal entrance of the evening. She had changed her costume; she was wearing a white robe now, with a large crown like so many icicles, and it crossed my mind that she resembled the fairy-tale Snow Queen. She was flanked by her surgeon and, I saw, Fire. My stomach gave an involuntary lurch. Fire was staring straight ahead, unseeing. It was all I could do to stop myself running through the crowd to get at her. As if to counter this very contingency, the trio were all but surrounded by a cadre of armed guards.

Trevellion spoke into a microphone. 'Ladies and gentlemen, I thank you for your patience, which I assure you will be well rewarded. The event is about to commence. If you would be so kind as to follow me . . .' She stepped from the patio and, with Fire and the surgeon in tow, cut a swath through the crowd and disappeared between the shrubbery and statuary.

I was about to follow the procession when I saw, beside the footbridge which connected the garden to the next valley, the tall, intimidating figure of Director Steiner. He was standing very still, a statuesque silhouette against the flaring aurora of Brightside. He seemed intent on the progress of the audience towards the amphitheatre. There was no sign of Weller.

Doug saw the direction of my gaze. He gripped my arm. 'Bob . . . Don't be so bloody stupid! If Weller sees you—'

'I want to know what's going on,' I said. I shook off his hand and hurried away over the lawn.

I paused before Steiner – or rather *beneath* him – and it was some time before he deigned to notice my presence. He was lost in some digitalized reality of his augmentation; hieroglyphs sequenced across the carotid spar of his occipital implant. His eyes were glazed.

'Benedict?' he said at last.

'What's going on, Steiner?' I asked.

He turned his gaze from contemplation of Trevellion's guards to me. 'That depends on what you know, Benedict,' he said. He turned and strolled across the bridge, and something in his pace suggested that he was inviting me to join him. I did so, catching him up and matching his pace. We left the bridge and passed behind the stand of fir trees which concealed the meadow. 'Well?' he asked at last.

'I know Weller was responsible for the deaths of Abe and Rodriguez,' I said.

I was relieved when he stopped and stared at me. He sighed. 'I don't expect you to believe me, Benedict – but I had no say in the matter. I am not a killer, and their deaths pain me. Not that this will help them, or you . . .' He began walking again.

'Who does Weller work for, Steiner? Earth, or Meridian? Or are they both in it together?'

We had paused beside a gap in the fir trees. To my right I could just make out the broad upper sweep of the meadow's far bank. To my left was a long drop to the star-silvered ocean. As we stood there, side by side in a silence that seemed to last for ever, I noticed movement in the periphery of my vision. Across the sea, perhaps kilometres distant, I made out the approach of a large helicopter. As yet, the sound of it had not reached us. Steiner had turned and was staring as if in an upright coma. He seemed all but physically removed. At last he snapped out of it and spoke briefly into his handset. He turned and looked through the gap in the trees, across the meadow at the phalanx of guards which occupied the same position on the opposite bank. 'Steiner?'

He seemed surprised that I was still beside him; he looked down condescendingly. 'Benedict, this is bigger than both you and me. If I told you . . .' he gazed out across the steadily filling amphitheatre, distracted for a second, 'and it got back to my superiors, then they would have no compunction about eliminating you.' He stopped there, and I thought I detected emotion in his tone as he went on, 'Look what happened to Abe Cunningham . . . I told him, I warned him that if what I told him got back to Weller—'

'What happened?' I whispered.

Steiner closed his eyes. 'Cunningham didn't listen to me, Benedict. Either that, or he didn't believe me. He confronted Weller. He didn't repeat everything I'd told him . . . But he said enough to convince Weller he knew too much and was dangerous—'

He stooped suddenly and swung in a quick about-turn, as if in response to some message from his computer implant. He stared out to sea.

I received the subliminal impression, then, that something, I had no idea what, was about to happen. The number of Trevellion's guards on duty, the approaching helicopter, the Director's strange behaviour . . .

'What is it?' I asked, urgency in my tone.

'Let's just say that I have a little score to settle before I leave Meridian.'

'A score?' I repeated, surprised. 'You're planning to disrupt Trevellion's event?'

Before I could find out, a blinding bolt of laser light flashed from the firs and hit Steiner in the chest. It deflected from his augmented breast-plate, ricocheted back and scored my ribcage like a lance of red-hot iron. I cried out and fell to the ground. As I lay there, dazed with pain, I saw Steiner take off. He ran from the path and into the cover of the fir trees: a second bolt followed him, striking timber, and I was gladdened by his escape. I was half aware of movement behind me, as Trevellion's guards broke cover and gave chase, shadowy figure against the dark boles of the trees. I tried to determine how badly I was injured. My fingers touched the drilled furrow. There seemed to be very little blood – the laser had cauterized the wound on the way through – but the pain was excruciating.

From my position on the path, sprawled out on my uninjured side, I had a perfect view over the cliff and out to sea. The helicopter lumbered towards the coastline, nose down – its arrival yet another component in a mystery far beyond my understanding. It hovered over the rocks of the foreshore, and I made out dark figures in its exit hatch, preparing to jump.

Then, before they could do so, a bright spoke of laser fire flashed out from amid the rocks below me. The bolt clipped the helicopter's starboard engine-cowling, and shards of disintegrating machinery spun away and out into the night, turning over and over in slow motion. I made out the Telemass Organization logo on the flank of the 'copter as it hung lopsidedly, lost its fight to remain airborne and slumped the two metres into the shallows. Small, dark figures swarmed out, their progress to shore impeded by the depth of the ocean and the treacherous rocks. Within seconds, more laser fire hailed through the darkness, both from the rocks below and from the clifftop. The bolts homed in remorselessly on the stricken 'copter and the floundering figures. The vehicles exploded under the onslaught, the roiling haemorrhage of flame followed by a muffled crump. The sudden illumination made the ongoing carnage all the more graphic; Trevellion's guards were picking off the invasion force with contemptuous ease. I saw bodies fall, lacerated, one by one until there were no more to target – and perhaps two minutes after the first bolt was fired, the skirmish was over. The sea extinguished the burning 'copter, and the waves washed over the rocks and the bodies below. Soon, nothing but the burned-out carcass of the 'copter remained to evidence the fact of the abortive invasion.

I closed my eyes, aware again of the pain in my side. I lay like a victim of the carnage below, caught on the cusp between the end of one dramatic occurrence and the beginning of another. I tried to make sense of Steiner's offensive, connect it to the happenings of the past few days. It struck me as odd that the invasion should have coincided with Trevellion's latest event. It became imperative that I should witness it.

Unable to stand, I pushed myself up the bank towards the gap in the trees, taking an age to move just three metres. I paused, a head's length from being able to see over the brow, then made one last desperate push. The length of my body scraped painfully over sand, rocks and pine cones. The glare of the will-o'-the-wisp lanterns came into view, dazzling me. I sagged, one cheek against the ground, breathing hard. Then, my eyesight becoming accustomed to the brightness, I lifted my head and stared down into the performance area.

Fire was standing very still on a circular grav-platform in the centre of the greensward, floating a metre above the ground. Her stance suggested apathy, or a drug-induced stupor. Her head was bowed and her arms hung limply by her sides.

Below her, the audience sprawled on scattered cushions and sunken foam-forms, looking up past Fire to where the open front of the floating stage was illuminated suddenly by a great block of golden light which spilled out across the greensward. The chattering spectators fell silent. I found myself holding my breath in anticipation.

As I watched, a small figure appeared on the golden stage. Shambling and hunched, he padded to the edge and looked out, down the ramp of light. Then he stepped off the stage and descended through the air. He was an ape-man, covered in hair and clutching a wooden club. Others soon followed him – small, trotting figures who hurried from the stage and deployed themselves around the perimeter of the greensward, crouching in wait. One readied himself in the air a metre from me, and its solidity, its reality, said much for Trevellion's talent. Down below, a spotlight was on Fire, and she was reciting her mother's poetry in a low voice, too faint for me to hear.

Then, from the stage, burst a herd of mammoths, with a speed and ferocity that alarmed me. A manufactured wind blew across the performance area, carrying the rank stench of the beasts, and the illusion of reality was heightened by the sound of their drumming gallop as they charged down the incline. Almost upon me, the leading mammoth fell and disappeared, and the ape-men emerged and cast spears and stones into the invisible pit.

While this was going on, yet more figures appeared and stepped from the stage, Egyptians flanked by distinct, towering statuary. There followed a series of set pieces featuring a succession of ancient races, each one emerging, playing out their story, and fading to make way for the next champion of civilization in the course of humanity's evolution. We were treated to scenes from the long history of *Homo sapiens*; from Egyptian to Chinese, Greek to Roman, and then the wonders of the modern world: the industrialization of Earth, the fusion age, the halcyon period of the post-nuclear era, to the miracles of the present day. All this was commented upon by Fire, reciting her mother's magnum opus, and though I could not make out the individual words, the sight alone was wonder enough.

As the last scene faded, a spotlight picked out the grav-platform on which Fire stood as it rose into the air. She intoned: 'In Earth, jewel of the Expansion / We share a heritage . . .' She continued, but either the speakers were not directed towards me, or the pain distracted my attention: I made out only the odd word. The platform sank again and the aerial display continued.

The theme of the second act was the conquest of space. From the stage emerged the immense length of an early multi-stage rocket. Startled gasps and cries of delight came from the crowd as the spaceship exploded into the night sky, as seemingly real as if it were a thing of steel and fire, and not just a brilliant projection. I was deafened by the thunder of its engines, even felt the heat sweep over me as it overflew the bank on which I lay. Then other craft issued from the stage, and we watched a procession of vessels from the early days of humanity's exploration of space; the first primitive lunar vessels, poignant in their antiquity, the manned Martian probes, the exploration smallships to the closer stars. Then came the bigships which carried colonists to the newly discovered habitable planets, vessels the size of city blocks which moved through the *nada*-continuum with the unhurried grace of all colossal objects; 'ships with evocative names like *The Pride of Madras, Remembrance of Things Past, The Satori Express* . . . As the last bigship faded, its place was taken by the technology that had superseded these leviathans of the space lanes: we watched Telemass stations beaming out bolts of demolecularized cargo from Earth to the many enclaves of life around the Expansion.

The spotlight found Fire, and she recited: 'We conquered Earth and / Our ambition Unconquered / We claimed the stars . . .' She continued, singing the praises of humankind's achievements, our inexorable shaping and forming of the great historical processes which culminated in the conquest of the stars. I strained to make out every word, but it was obvious that I was slipping in and out of consciousness – coming to my senses, startled by an amplified phrase or sudden burst of illumination, only to slip back against my will into troubled darkness, where words and images merged in a nightmarish alternative to what was happening above. It came to me, in my delirium, that so small a figure as Fire must surely be crushed by the recital of so much historical fact. Was this what Trevellion had had in mind, the desire to crush Fire's spirit with a display of her own art and erudition, and for me to witness it? Then, quite suddenly, I would come to my senses, and the nightmare would fade, and I would realize that I was projecting my own fears, my own terror at being overwhelmed by the weight and significance of past events (perhaps rooted in my part in history's worst space disaster) upon Fire. During periods of lucidity I tried to shake this nightmare fear, but even then vague horror and apprehension lurked in the back of my mind. At one point I passed out for what seemed like hours, only to be awoken by a flash of light.

The night sky was transformed into a series of stunning panoramas, each one quite unlike the last. I gathered that these were scenes from the many colony worlds. I looked out across a rain-forested delta and a quicksilver sea; plains of crimson sand spangled with spherical living domes; water-worlds bearing floating pontoon megalopoleis . . .

As the scenes changed, Fire intoned words familiar to me, 'I stand as one deserted / An alien upon Alien soil . . .' The aerial display now presented various scenes from across our own planet, and so real were they that I felt I had been transported physically. I saw landscapes of Brightside, the furthest reaches to which unmanned probes had ventured without destruction: molten rivers, white hot, ran into great steaming oceans of magma abubble and aflame. Then came further scenes, each one a little more temperate than the last, until zone blue appeared and the cool shores of the meridional sea. Then the display showed a succession of scenes from the frozen, inimical wastes of Darkside. The first, in complete contrast to Brightside's hellish inferno, presented a hostile vision of mammoth glaciers and vast ice-sheets reflecting the unwinking light of the stars . . . The overall effect, from the conflagration of Brightside to the frigidity of Darkside, was that the planet of Meridian was too hostile a home for a species as unadaptable as humankind, and that the meagre points of habitable terrain, which did support life, did so in defiance of the mighty, mindless, alien forces at work on either hemisphere . . . Against this melancholy scene, Fire lamented in plaintive tones the place of humanity on Meridian – and this vision of our insignificance complemented my own nightmares of personal failure, and I slipped once again into unconsciousness, my mind full of the fires of hell and the frozen void of space to which I had consigned one hundred innocent victims.

When I came to my senses, the aerial display was fading. The illumination died and the spotlight fixed on the hovering grav-platform winked out. The guests stood as one and cheered, and the cheer was taken up and repeated, carried across the greensward in a great appreciative roar. At last the guests began to drift from the meadow, return to the garden to resume their drinking and conversation, eager to applaud the genius of Tamara Trevellion.

Minutes elapsed. I felt a curious sense of anti-climax. Then the spotlight snapped on again, presenting the platform to an empty greensward as it sank to ground level. Fire was a tiny, exhausted figure seated cross-legged with her head bowed almost into the bowl of her lap. Slowly, then, she raised her head, and I saw that she was looking into one of the six vid-cameras floating beside the platform. She climbed wearily to her feet, gestured, declaimed to the camera, clearly still performing, her words no longer amplified and thus lost in the distance between us. Only then did I notice the one remaining spectator. Seated directly below me, upright on a foam-form, was Tamara Trevellion. She was leaning forward, watching intently, and her posture indicated a sense of anticipation which at once froze and frightened me.

Was it my imagination, or did Fire look up then, with an expression of torture on her perfect face? I even imagined that I saw tears in

her eyes. With all my strength I raised my head and called, 'Fire!'
but weakly, so that she might hardly have heard me. As I watched,
consciousness dwindling, I heard my cry repeated, at first thinking
it an echo. Then I saw, sprinting from the darkness surrounding the
platform, the figure of Wolfe Steiner. He dived in one last frantic
effort to reach her – and I was with him, our enmity forgotten, willing
him to succeed on my behalf.

By the evidence of the laser bolts which flashed from the darkness,
half a dozen guards were lying in wait. The electric-blue shafts
formed a matrix which skewered the Director. I covered my eyes to
be spared the sight of his death, but could not shut out the crackle
of laser on flesh and the sickly sweet stench which resulted.

Down below, Tamara Trevellion was on her feet.

On the platform, Fire stared at Steiner's shredded remains in
disbelief. She turned from the sight and, as if against her will, stepped
down and walked across the greensward. I cried out again, oblivious
of danger. Fire paused. For long seconds she looked up at me, her
mind filled with who knows what terror and regret. Then with the
fatalism of the damned she calmly knelt and switched something set
into the ground. She stood and turned. Five metres before her a
trap-door lifted automatically to reveal a subterranean chamber. Even
then I wanted to deny what I knew was about to happen.

The sand lion emerged, paused and stared at Fire. I thought for
an incredible second that it was about to forgo the imperative of its
kind and ignore the girl – then I saw Trevellion move below me.
She was holding something, a mechanical device of some kind. The
sand lion advanced, tossing its barbarous head of horns. It opened
its jaws in a roar that stilled my heart. I attempted to stand, but the
pain allowed me only as far as my knees. Then it was all I could do
to remain conscious and watch as the lion charged. Fire tried to run;
I could see the terror on her face as she willed herself to countermand
her drug-induced instructions, but she was mired to the spot like a
figure in a nightmare.

The lion leapt, dashed her small body to the ground, and I cried
out in rage and anguish.

It was daylight by the time I came to my senses.

I lay face down on the grass, the events of the night before swamping me in the seconds it took to regain full consciousness. I kept my eyes closed against the glare of the sunlight – but the real reason was that I did not want to witness the remains of last night's event. When I did open my eyes, some macabre fascination made me look over the edge and down into the performance area. To my surprise, it was empty. There was no sign of the stage, the grav-platform or the trap-door to the underground chamber. I climbed unsteadily to my feet, my ribcage throbbing. Regardless of the danger, should any of Trevellion's guards see me, I made my way down the bank to the greensward.

I was obviously still in shock: that was the only explanation for my ability to cross the grass to the place where mere hours ago Fire had lost her life, and stare in bewilderment around the arena. I turned to where I had seen Director Steiner fall, but there was no sign of his remains, either. Still in a daze, I left the greensward and came to the garden. I was still too overcome with numbed incomprehension to think of revenge, and the only reason I made my way to the dome was that it was a link to a far better past. Perhaps part of me thought that I might even find Fire, hiding in her room. I tried to convince myself that the finale of last night's performance had been nothing more than a macabre trick with screens and projectors . . .

I entered the dome. A strange silence hung about the place. I moved through the rooms and made my way down the connecting passage to Fire's bed-chamber. Nothing remained to suggest that it had once belonged to her. I told myself that I could just detect, elusive and tantalizing, the aroma of her scent in the air. As the many memories of my time with Fire returned to me, I could no longer shut out the final, terrible vision, and for the first time I began to apprehend the tortured complexity of Tamara Trevellion's motivations. I wondered if I would ever come to fully understand what had happened, and *why* it had happened – and, if not, then how I would be able to go on living in ignorance.

I retraced my steps. I came to the lounge and stopped dead. There, by the exit, stood Tamara Trevellion. Her fins shimmered about her slender body, giving her the aspect of an apparition. 'When the ultimate event is achieved,' she said, her voice reaching me from a distance, 'I shall take great delight in destroying all these . . . these *objects*.'

I rushed towards her, and as Trevellion disappeared, a ghost in my imagination, I noticed for the first time the remains of her works of art. They stood on their pedestals in the empty room, sculptures in crystal and wood reduced to slag and cinder – the desecration a testament to her ultimate achievement.

FIRE

In the days that followed I kept to my dome and had no contact at all with the outside world. I shunned the vid-screen, even the entertainment channels; I wanted to be alone with my thoughts. In my isolation, I could almost persuade myself that what had happened that night on Trevellion's island was nothing more than an hallucination, a nightmare scenario far more terrible than reality could ever be. Of course, another part of me knew the truth; when I had almost succeeded in convincing myself that Fire was still alive, her continued non-presence, and flash visions of the sand lion's attack, told me otherwise ... Even then, when I came finally to accept the fact of Fire's death, my reactions were erratic. I could recall the times we had spent together, and feel gladdened that we had done so; then, for no reason at all, a small thing like the recollection of her smile, of her moccasin lying in the sand, would send me into fits of tearful grief.

I took to sitting for long periods on the patio and staring out across the sea. Abe's island in the foreground, and Trevellion's beyond, a faint blur on the horizon, were constant reminders of my loss. I told myself that by regarding them day after day I might come to some psychological acceptance of what had happened. I did not, however, dwell on Tamara Trevellion: I tried to shut out thoughts of the woman from my mind, for fear that notions of revenge might prove all-consuming and, in time, self-destructive. On the few occasions that my thoughts did dwell on her, I frightened myself with the power of my ability to feel hatred.

One morning, perhaps five days after the event, I was seated as usual on the patio, looking out across the ocean for the ferry. For

155

the past few days I had used the punctual passing of the hydrofoil as a reminder to go to the kitchen and feed myself. Today it had neither passed the island on its way down to Main, nor on its return trip back up the archipelago. I was speculating idly over the reason for this when I saw a launch appear from an island beyond Trevellion's and score a long parabolic wake across the bright blue surface of the ocean. I estimated that if the vehicle's wake was to form a perfect semi-circle, then the launch's destination would have to be my island.

I watched the launch decelerate and drift into the cove, wondering who my visitor might be. Now, with Fire and Abe and Doug all gone, I knew no one likely to pay me a social call. I watched the short, stocky man climb from the launch, peer up the hillside to the dome with a hand shielding his eyes, and begin the long ascent.

Five minutes later he rounded the last bend and approached the patio, and I belatedly recognized him. Individuals present a different aspect out of uniform, and Trevellion's guard, Tanner – the same who had taken Fire from me that day on Abe's island – looked almost human in casual slacks and a chequered shirt.

Already I was on my feet. I believe, had I been armed then, that I would have shot him without a second thought. 'What the hell —'

He stopped short in response to my anger, held up both hands. 'Careful, Benedict . . .' Without the authority of his uniform or side-arm, and perhaps aware that my rage was justified, he was conciliatory.

'How dare you come here' – I spluttered – 'after what you did . . .'

He was shaking his head. 'I did nothing, Benedict. When I found out what was happening, I got out. I haven't worked for Trevellion since before the event.'

'If you expect me to believe—'

'I have something for you, Benedict.'

I hardly heard him. 'Where's Trevellion?'

Tanner shook his head. 'I've no idea. She moved to some other island, way down the chain. I don't know where.'

I calmed, taking deep breaths, but at the same time feeling something building up inside me. He was the first person I had spoken to since that night, the first outside verification I had received that what I had witnessed was not some gross hallucination. It was as if he were the harbinger of dire news, and I hated him for it.

'What do you want?'

'Fire made this before she . . . before the event.' From the breast pocket of his shirt he produced a small silver vid-disc. He held it out to me. I noticed that his hand was shaking. 'She gave it to me and asked me to deliver it to you . . .' He looked at the disc. 'I said I would. I haven't played it. I couldn't bring myself to . . . so I don't know what's on it.' He stepped forward, holding out the disc and staring me in the eye with an expression that might have been pitiful.

I stood rooted to the spot, unable to respond. The fact that Fire had thought to contact me in her last hours, and the fear of what the disc might contain, produced in me an ambivalent response: I wanted more than anything to take the recording, to re-establish contact with Fire, but at the same time I did not want to be destroyed by the grief I had so far held in check.

Tanner took another step forward. 'Please, take it. She begged me to give it to you. She said you'd understand . . .'

I reached out and took the disc, inclining my head in silent thanks.

I watched him retrace his steps down to the cove, the disc heavy in my hand. Only when the launch started up and accelerated from the island did I step inside and cross the lounge to the vid-screen. Even then I delayed still further, staring at the blank screen in a bid to postpone the inevitable.

As I slipped the disc into the drive, felt it snap home, I was aware of the rush of my pulse in my ears. I concentrated on the screen to the exclusion of all else. I had the sudden urge to withdraw and destroy the disc – so I tapped the start key before I gave into the impulse.

The picture flickered, strobed bars of black and white, then cleared. Fire sat in her bedroom. All I could see was her head and shoulders. She was reaching out to the recorder, making adjustments. Then she sat back and stared into the screen. She was wearing the white gown, and her hair was braided and coiled about her head. She looked alert. Evidently she had made this recording just before the surgeon had drugged her for the very last time.

I stared at her pale oval face, the pointed chin, the dark bar of her eyebrows and her short blonde fringe high on her forehead. She appeared calm, composed. Only when she spoke did she betray her fear, her apprehension. She looked about her, through the walls of her dome, checking to ensure she was unobserved, before beginning. 'Bob – I haven't got long . . . A guard said he'd take this to you so . . . Well, you'll know all that already. You'll also know . . .' She stopped there, biting her bottom lip to prevent the tears. 'But there's nothing I can do to get away. They've got the island surrounded. Tamara will be here soon with her surgeon.' She stopped there, and when she went on she was contrite. 'It worked, Bob – the frost.' She stared down at her fingers, whispered, 'I know why Tamara blocked my memory of Jade's death.'

She leaned forward then, gripped the edge of the table in determination. 'Are you listening, Bob?' she said, her emerald eyes burning. 'I also know why Hannah Rodriguez was killed. She knew too much. She told Tamara and I overheard them . . .'

Then Fire unburdened herself and, in doing so, made the terrible events of the past week perfectly clear.

I boarded my launch and headed for Main Island . . .

I made the journey not so much to verify what Fire had told me – a simple call through to the island itself would have achieved that – but to distance myself from the vid-disc. My initial impulse, when Fire had reached out and stopped the recording, was to take the disc and burn it. I knew, however, that I would live to regret it. In due course, when the pain had passed and I had worked through my grief, the recording would stand as testimony of our time together. To have destroyed it now would be in a way to have destroyed the events through which we had lived, our shared experiences. It would be unbearably painful to view the disc in years to come, but beyond the tragedy I could take comfort that Fire had made the recording at all, that she had thought enough about me not to leave me in ignorance.

As I approached the wide harbour of Main Island, uppermost in my mind was not so much *what* Fire had told me, but the *way* she had told it. Throughout she had shown courage before the knowledge of her death, she had faced me bravely and told me what she knew, aware that if she had broken down, shown, however briefly, her true emotions, the resulting recording would have been even more heart-wrenching than it was already.

As for *what* she had told me, it would take some time to adjust to this – like my grief, it was something that would take years to come to terms with, and even then might not be something I could ever wholly accept. As I drove slowly through the streets of Main, I thought I detected a subtle difference about the place. True, there were fewer people about – which was to be expected – but the difference I noticed was in the attitude of the citizens who remained. They seemed friendlier, unified in the face of adversity. People gathered on street corners to discuss the situation, congregated in front gardens. When I stopped at a station for a recharge, the attendant, a total stranger, smiled in greeting as if I were a regular customer: his smile told me that we were allies, ranged against an injustice about which we could do nothing. For the first time in the history of Meridian, we faced an uncertain future.

I made my way to the Telemass station. I passed a crowd in a parking lot, quietly staring up at a great screen showing a live broadcast from the Governor's residence. The deputy Governor exhorted the populace to keep calm, work together in the face of what he called the terrible treachery. I stopped and listened for a while: the deputy claimed that he had been told nothing – which was probably true enough, as he was still here – and that no blame should be attributed to the officials who remained. He counselled solidarity and perseverance, spoke rousingly of the years of hard work ahead for every citizen on Meridian ... I gunned the engine and crossed the suspension bridge to the station.

I was not alone. It seemed that perhaps half the population of the island had had the same idea, as if to verify for themselves that the station was defunct, inoperable. It rose, grand and majestic against the clear blue sky, a towering epitaph to a sequestered people. A hundred vehicles were parked around the scimitar tripod, and citizens strolled aimlessly, uncertain exactly how to respond now that they had reached their destination. The elevator was working, and it shuttled groups of quiet sightseers from the base of the station to the operations' platform. I took my place in line and presently rode with a dozen other colonists to the deck. Here, islanders wandered about in reflective silence, the liberty to walk where before had been off-limits tempered by the solemnity of the occasion.

At one end of the deck, a crowd had gathered around a small screen. I made my way over to it and eased through the press. I was shocked to see the face of Wolfe Steiner, speaking to us from a recording made in preparation for the shut-down. This recording reminded me too much of the one I had fled, and I found my throat blocked with emotion. Director Steiner was doing his best to justify the wholesale shutdown of the colony planet Meridian 673. 'It pains me to repeat . . .' was one of his phrases. 'We must face up to the harsh reality,' he said, and I recalled his ultimate sacrifice and wondered if, had he lived, he would have left the planet, or remained and faced the consequences. 'Meridian is an unprofitable planet, and Earth can no longer subsidize Meridian and over two dozen other similar colonies across the Expansion. Against my wishes, and those of certain members of the council, the decision was taken to close down the Telemass operations on Meridian. The stations on twenty-six other planets will also be closed. It was deemed impossible to repatriate the entire populations, some one billion citizens, of these planets. I personally regret this decision, and can only counsel . . .' He continued, saying nothing about the fact that Meridian relied on regular food supplies from Earth to survive – but his knowledge of the omission showed in the strain on his face.

When Steiner came to the end of his speech, his place was taken on the screen by a grey-suited official. He announced a series of public meetings to take place on various islands of the archipelago over the next few days, to assess the position, elect governing bodies and appoint officials to oversee the development programme. One fool cheered, and this provoked applause from the other viewers.

I left them to it and made my way over to the elevator. A minute later I stepped into the parking lot and crossed to my launch. The proximity of so many people, concerned with only one thing and ignorant of Fire's death, accentuated my sense of isolation and loss. I gunned the engine and drove quickly across the suspension bridge. Soon I was out on the open sea and heading for the sanctuary of my own island.

The drone of the engine, the thump of the hull against the surface of the ocean, hypnotized me. Fire's face appeared again in my mind's eye, and I could do nothing to banish it. I heard her last words in my head.

'Steiner's no fool, Bob. He knows what kind of woman Tamara is, he knows how psychologically tortured she is. He was close to Jade – he guessed what really happened to her, and he could see Tamara doing the same to me. That's why he wanted me to leave with him. He told me that I was in danger if I stayed on the island, that Jade's death was more than just an accident . . . Even then, I thought he meant that Tamara's cruelty had pressured Jade into killing herself, not that she had actually . . .' Fire had paused there, gathering herself. 'Do you see now why I had to have the frost? Do you understand? I just had to find out what really happened to her!' She paused again, then continued. 'Now that I know . . . know for certain what really took place . . . I wish I didn't—' The knowledge of what was about to happen to her had been plain to see on her face, and it broke my heart.

I steered the launch in beside the jetty and just sat there for a long time, gripping the wheel and staring at nothing, just seeing Fire's stricken face high in the sky.

She had finished, 'I know I used you, Bob . . . But at the same time – if things could have been different, if only . . .' And she had lifted her head and smiled bravely through her tears, and then reached out and brought the communication to an end before she broke down completely.

Later, drunk and maudlin, the events of the past few days going around and around in my head, it occurred to me that Fire had explained everything, everything except just one thing. Why had Tamara Trevellion kept the knowledge of the planet's shut-down to herself, and not made the fact public?

The answer was so obvious, really, that I completely failed to see it.

I found out the following day.

10

'BETRAYAL'

I awoke late as usual, dragged myself to the kitchen and made a mug
of coffee. I drank it in the lounge, staring out at the islands. Something moved me to switch on the vid-screen and try to find a news
channel, my social apathy giving way to a desire to know how the
business of saving the world was progressing. I switched from one
band of static to the next, wondering if the situation had deteriorated
to the extent that the authorities were unable to put out even a simple
news bulletin. Then I chanced upon a moving picture.

It was terribly familiar.

I sat, unable to move, and stared at the procession of images on
the wall-screen. The pictures were accompanied by a voice intoning
poetry, Fire's voice. I watched, appalled and yet fascinated, as the
history of Earth was played out before my eyes. These images were
intercut with simple, stark shots of Fire, standing to attention on the
grav-platform, reciting lines of verse.

Then the images switched from those of Earth and spaceflight, to
those of far-flung colonies and Meridian. I watched the familiar
progression of Brightside landscapes through to the frozen vistas
of Darkside, culminating with shots of the meridian sea and the
archipelago, caught in the planetary vice of the two inimical hemispheres. Tamara Trevellion's poetry emphasized the inhospitability
of the colony world. 'We rode the wave of the Push / Settling words
not meant for humankind . . .' Fire's voice, the close-up of her face,
her tears, brought a cry of rage from me. I knew, then, what was to
happen next. For the audience that night, the event had finished
here. But this recorded vid-art would go beyond the live event and
show what only Tamara Trevellion and I had seen. Fire recited

the lines, 'Betrayed, we are made isolate / Twenty light-years from home / On a world hostile and unforgiving.' Intercut with the full-length images of Fire, alone in the darkness, fear visible on her face, were shots of a stalking sand lion, alien and evil. A doom-laden soundtrack heightened the tension, the separate images of girl and lion edited together in quick succession to unbearable effect. I tried to close my eyes as the music crescendoed, but found myself unable to do so. The sand lion leapt. The girl – no longer Fire, but some perfect personification of humankind – screamed as the beast tore her limb from limb. This was shown in a series of quick shots from every angle, the image never remaining long enough for the effect to be sickening. Her death, seen this way in a thousand protracted cuts – and not over with in seconds as it was in reality – made the scene all the more horrific, the moral of the piece all the more shocking. In Trevellion's view, humanity on Meridian would die slowly, left to starve to death by a callous central authority.

The last frame – of Fire's wide, dead eyes staring accusingly into the camera – faded, to be replaced with the caption: *'Betrayal –* VidArt by Tamara Trevellion.' Then this too faded, to be replaced by images of Earth's history, and Fire's voice, beginning the cycle all over again, as Trevellion's event was beamed from Meridian, across the light-years to a suitably chastened Earth.

I reached out and switched off the screen. I sat in silence for a long time, trying to work out my reaction to what I had seen. I felt sickened, and the feeling had to do not only with the horrific content of the video, but with the realization of its quality.

There could be no doubt that *Betrayal* was Tamara Trevellion's greatest work of art. I suspected that it would be judged as such by those on Earth and Meridian who viewed it without knowing the full story behind its production. Perhaps only I was in a position to judge the piece, to understand the artist's motives. I alone knew that what had driven her to produce *Betrayal* was not so much indignation or anger at Earth's treachery, or an altruistic desire to speak out on behalf of the citizens of Meridian denied a voice. Tamara Trevellion had been consumed by the need to sacrifice that which was close to her, her daughter – who she hated, as she was unable to hate herself – at the altar of Art in a bid to appease the devil within which taunted her for the failures of her past. She had attempted this with Jade, but in her own estimation had failed; and she had tried again with Fire . . .

For two days following my first viewing of *Betrayal*, I wanted nothing more than to track down Tamara Trevellion and kill her. I thought of nothing else. It seemed to me that the scales of universal good and evil were forever tipped in favour of the latter while Tamara Trevellion remained alive. To make the world a better place, to balance the scales, it was my duty to eradicate her.

Then it came to me with the impact of a revelation that revenge was unnecessary. As I sat on the patio one evening, watching the shield usher in another period of darkness, I understood the truth. I realized that, by their very nature, artists are forever dissatisfied. They are only as good as their last creation, and when the satisfaction of achievement begins to wane, when time has intervened to show them that their last work is not as great as they hoped, that it can be improved upon, then they are driven to produce something which, in their eyes at least, is even greater. And so on. This is the axiom of artistic endeavour. Tamara Trevellion had used first Jade, and then Fire, in her art – and, I knew, no matter how fine she considered her latest creation, there would come a time when satisfaction wore thin, when the need would arise to create again . . . Now Trevellion had only herself to hate, and it occurred to me that by leaving her to the self-destructive processes of her art I would be gaining the ultimate act of revenge. I foresaw a time when Tamara Trevellion would either kill herself in despair at having no one else to hate, or be forced to confront her self-hatred and produce, in one sado-masochistic burst of creative energy – which might even then prove suicidal – a work of art which would truly be of herself and acclaimed as great, and by so doing make some amends for all the misery and suffering for which she was responsible.

The sense of no longer feeling hatred was like a balm.

At night, after a day fishing or working in the fields, I sit on the patio and watch the pterosaurs fly to Brightside. The sight always fills me with sadness and regret, and reminds me as well of Fire, who wanted so much to escape, but never did.

Every night I think of all the frost on Brightside, just waiting to be taken. Then I contemplate the events which have brought me here, and what the drug turned me into, and I put all thoughts of frost from my mind.

I survive. I live from day to day, wishing at times that I had never known Fire Trevellion, had never suffered all the pain, while at others realizing, of course, that all the pain was necessary.

Terry Bisson
Voyage to the Red Planet £4.99

WINNER OF THE HUGO AND NEBULA AWARDS

In the not so distant future, the US Government, bankrupt and desperate, has auctioned off its agencies to private enterprise. NASA is now a Disney subsidiary; the Nixon Orbital Space Station is a family theme park. Space still hides some secrets, and one of them is about to be launched on an unsuspecting public: the Mars ship, *Mary Poppins*, built before the market crash and secreted in high orbit.

Movie moghul Markson uses fast talk, creative accounting and out-and-out blackmail to *persuade* two of the original Mars team to pilot the spacecraft on her maiden voyage to Mars. With two bona fide certified Hollywood Stars, and a brilliant – if eccentric – midget cinematographer, Markson plans to shoot The Movie of All Time . . .

"Damn. What a writer"
Ed Bryant

"Superb . . . every detail is telling, painting a vivid picture of an all-too-possible future"
Locus

"Mars, a movie set and astronauts for extras! Terry Bisson strikes again, illuminating us with his rock 'n' roll anarchist sensibility, making it plain that the answer to all the Big Questions is None of the Above. Better check your dicktracy and climb aboard the *Mary Poppins*. This is one trip you don't want to miss"
Lucius Shepard